OLYMPIAD TRAINER

FOR MATHEMATICS

Standard - I

- Useful for Olympiads and other competitive exams like IPM, Wisdom etc.
- Ample number of questions on every topic.
- Helpful and informative explanations.
- Model Question Papers

By

Mrs. Kajal Sugandhi

NIRALI
PRAKASHAN
ADVANCEMENT OF KNOWLEDGE

N0011

OLYMPIAD TRAINER (STD. I : MATHEMATICS)   ISBN 978-93-5164-536-8

First Edition   :   **June 2015**

©   :   **Author**

Published By :
NIRALI PRAKASHAN
Abhyudaya Pragati, 1312, Shivaji Nagar,
Off J.M. Road, PUNE – 411005
Tel - (020) 25512336/37/39, Fax - (020) 25511379
Email : niralipune@pragationline.com

☞ DISTRIBUTION CENTRES

PUNE

Nirali Prakashan   :   119, Budhwar Peth, Jogeshwari Mandir Lane, Pune 411002, Maharashtra
Tel : (020) 2445 2044, 66022708, Fax : (020) 2445 1538
Email : bookorder@pragationline.com, niralilocal@pragationline.com

Nirali Prakashan   :   S. No. 28/27, Dhyari, Near Pari Company, Pune 411041
Tel : (020) 24690204 Fax : (020) 24690316
Email : dhyari@pragationline.com, bookorder@pragationline.com

MUMBAI

Nirali Prakashan   :   385, S.V.P. Road, Rasdhara Co-op. Hsg. Society Ltd.,
Girgaum, Mumbai 400004, Maharashtra
Tel : (022) 2385 6339 / 2386 9976, Fax : (022) 2386 9976
Email : niralimumbai@pragationline.com

☞ DISTRIBUTION BRANCHES

JALGAON

Nirali Prakashan   :   34, V. V. Golani Market, Navi Peth, Jalgaon 425001,
Maharashtra, Tel : (0257) 222 0395, Mob : 94234 91860

KOLHAPUR

Nirali Prakashan   :   New Mahadvar Road, Kedar Plaza, 1st Floor Opp. IDBI Bank
Kolhapur 416 012, Maharashtra. Mob : 9850046155

NAGPUR

Pratibha Book Distributors   :   Above Maratha Mandir, Shop No. 3, First Floor,
Rani Jhanshi Square, Sitabuldi, Nagpur 440012, Maharashtra
Tel : (0712) 254 7129

DELHI

Nirali Prakashan   :   4593/21, Basement, Aggarwal Lane 15, Ansari Road, Daryaganj
Near Times of India Building, New Delhi 110002
Mob : 08505972553

BENGALURU

Pragati Book House   :   House No. 1, Sanjeevappa Lane, Avenue Road Cross,
Opp. Rice Church, Bengaluru – 560002.
Tel : (080) 64513344, 64513355,Mob : 9880582331, 9845021552
Email:bharatsavla@yahoo.com

CHENNAI

Pragati Books   :   9/1, Montieth Road, Behind Taas Mahal, Egmore,
Chennai 600008 Tamil Nadu, Tel : (044) 6518 3535,
Mob : 94440 01782 / 98450 21552 / 98805 82331,
Email : bharatsavla@yahoo.com

niralipune@pragationline.com | www.pragationline.com

Also find us on f www.facebook.com/niralibooks

PREFACE

It gives me immense pleasure to present this book for **Mathematics Olympiads For Standard I.** Maths is a subject that has applications in all other subjects. Maths is needed for mundane everyday jobs as well as in highly technical fields. Therefore every parent wishes his or her child to excel in Maths.

Olympiad exams encourage children to apply the basic principles of Maths in situations that we encounter in every day life.

This book for Std I students has been prepared keeping in mind the basic mathematical concepts that the students are tested for in the Olympiads. Maximum efforts have have been made to see that the chapters are simplified and elaborated so that the child gets a better understanding of the concepts and the problems based on them. The main purpose of this book is to give thorough practise of all the possible questions to the child so that it becomes easier for him/her to ace the exams.

This book will not only help in preparing for the Olympiads but also for other competitive exams and regular academics.

The model papers included in the book recreate the exam like environment. Explanations are given for each and every question which I am sure will clear the doubts from the minds of the students.

Utmost care has been taken while preparing this book but any error that might have crept in by oversight is deeply regretted.

I take this opportunity to express my deep gratitude to my family members, especially my mother-in- law, Mrs. Geeta Sugandhi who has been my pillar of support without whose encouragement and strong belief in my abilities, this book would not have been possible.

I am thankful to Shri Dineshbhai Furia, Shri Jignesh Furia and the entire staff of Nirali Prakashan for their co-operation in bringing out this book.

Every valuable suggestion and constructive criticism that would help in the improvement of the book will be highly appreciated.

Author

Kajal Sugandhi

5th June 2015

CONTENTS

•••

MATHEMATICS – STANDARD I

Chapter 1
NUMBER SENSE

Topics:-Numbers and number names 1 to 100, ones and tens , greater than, less than and equal to, before, after and between numbers, one more than, one less than, ascending and descending order, smallest number, largest number, counting in 2's and 5's, represent numbers on the abacus, counting, counting numbers on abacus, ordinals.

Important points

Number sense - Descending order means arranging the numbers from the biggest number to smallest number.

Ascending order means arranging the numbers from smallest to biggest.

Choose the Correct Answer

1. What is the correct descending order of 74, 82, 56, 25?

    (A) 74, 25, 82, 56   (B) 25, 56, 74, 82

    (C) 82, 74, 56, 25   (D) None of these

2. Number after 49 is

    (A) 48   (B) 50   (C) 51   (D) 42

3. There are 6 ones and 3 tens in

    (A) 63   (B) 36   (C) 32   (D) 61

4. Which number is between 39 and 41?

    (39)   (   )   (41)

    (A) 42   (B) 38   (C) 40   (D) 44

5. What comes before 81?

    (A) 82   (B) 79   (C) 80   (D) 72

6. Which of the following is a correct match?

    (A) 32 – Thirty   (B) 46 – Forty six

    (C) 89 – Eighty Five   (D) 19 – Ninety One

7. What is the correct ascending order of 38, 83, 33, 88?

    (A) 88, 83, 38, 33   (B) 33, 38, 83, 88

    (C) 88, 38, 33, 83   (D) 33, 38, 88, 83

8. Number after 89 is

    (A) 98   (B) 90   (C) 91   (D) 88

9. 42 is same as

    (A) 4 + 2   (B) 40 – 2   (C) 40 + 2   (D) 41 – 2

10. What comes before 40?

    (A) 41   (B) 39   (C) 42   (D) 46

11. 59 is same as

    (A) 55+9   (B) 60-1   (C) 50+9   (D) Both B & C

12. Which statement is true?

    (A) Flowers are more than balls   (B) Balls are more than flowers

    (C) Balls are less than flowers   (D) Balls are equal to flowers.

13. Which box shows zero Δ in it ?

(A) 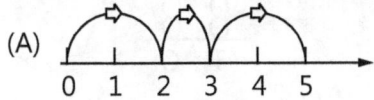   (B)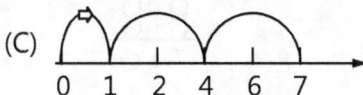

(C) [   ]   (D)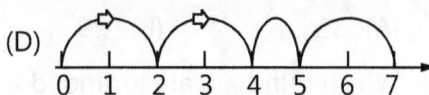

14. There are 8 ones and 9 tens in

(A) 89   (B) 98   (C) 80   (D) 90

15. Which number line shows counting in 2's?

(A)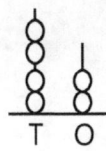
    0 1 2 3 4 5

(C)
    0 1 2 4 6 7

(B)
    0 1 2 3 4 5 6 7 8

(D)
    0 1 2 3 4 5 6 7

16. 7 tens + 4 ones is

(A) 47   (B) 74   (C) 77   (D) 44

17.

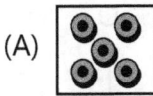   Shows
    T O

(A) 24   (B) 42   (C) 40   (D) 2

18. Which figure shows equal collection?

(A)   (B)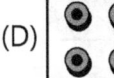

(C) 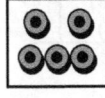   (D)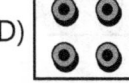

19. What comes after 99?

    (A) 98   (B) 90   (C) 100   (D) 91

20. Which abacus shows 1 more than 42?

    (A) 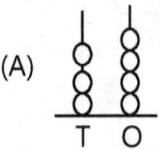   (B)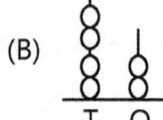

    (C) 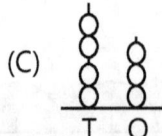   (D)

21. 1 less than 30 is

    (A) 31   (B) 29   (C) 32   (D) 28

22. Which numbers are arranged in descending order?

    (A) 42, 24, 74, 47   (B) 28, 31, 46, 92

    (C) 85, 72, 53, 49   (D) None of these.

23. Which star has a number more than 69 but less than 71?

    (A) ☆ 72   (B) ☆ 70

    (C) ☆ 68   (D) None of these.

24. Which abacus is 1 more than 29?

    (A) 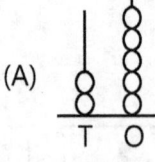   (B)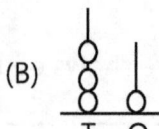

    (C) 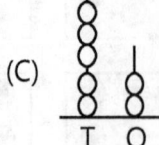   (D)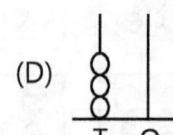

25. 1 more than 50 is

    (A) 49   (B) 52   (C) 51   (D) None of these

26. What will come in between?

    (A) 78   (B) 82   (C) 80   (D) 83

27. Which numbers are arranged in ascending order?

    (A) 4, 14, 94, 49   (B) 15, 81, 99, 90

    (C) 21, 42, 68, 94   (D) 99, 84, 23, 3.

28. 82 is same as

    (A) 83 – 1   (B) 81 + 2   (C) 80 – 2   (D) None of these.

29. Ninety two = ----------------

    a) 90   b) 29   c) 92   d) 20

30. 74 is same as

    (A) 7 tens and 4 ones   (B) 7 tens and 40 ones

    (C) 17 tens and 4 ones   (D) None of these.

31. Number after 39 is

    (A) 41   (B) 40   (C) 38   (D) 42

32.

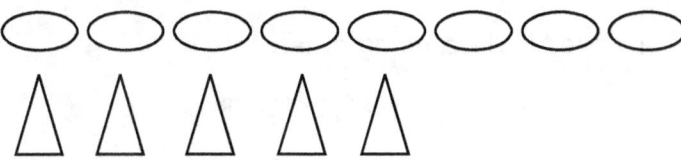

Which statement is true?

    (A) Ovals are less than triangles.   (B) Triangles are less than ovals.

    (C) Triangles are equal to ovals.   (D) Triangles are more than ovals.

33. Number before 80 is _____.

(A) 81   (B) 82   (C) 78   (D) 79

34. Which number line shows counting by 2's?

(A) 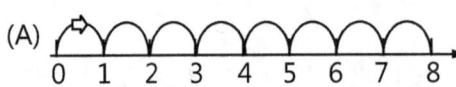   (C)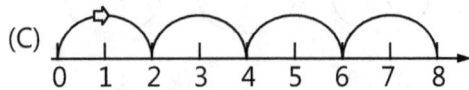

(B) 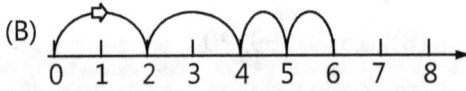   (D)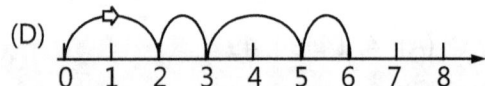

35. 89 is same as

(A) 80 + 9   (B) 89 + 9   (C) 70 + 9   (D) None of these.

36. Which abacus shows 1 more than 60?

(A) 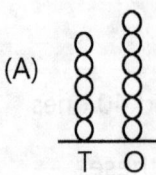   (B)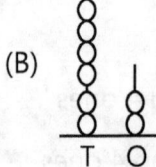

(C) 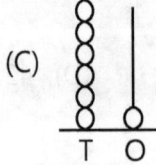   (D) None of these.

37. Which numbers are arranged in descending order?

(A) 13, 19, 91, 31   (B) 81, 24, 16, 3

(C) 42, 93, 81, 64   (D) 24, 36, 48, 72

38. There are 4 ones and 9 tens in

(A) 49   (B) 94   (C) 90   (D) 40

39. 7 one + 2 tens = _____

   (A) 70 + 2   (B) 20 + 7   (C) 27 + 2   (D) None of these

40. 8 ones + 2 tens = _____

   (A) 82   (B) 28   (C) 20   (D) 80

41. Which number comes between 69 and 71?

   (A) 68   (B) 72   (C) 66   (D) 70

42. The expanded form of 36 is

   (A) 30 tens + 60 ones   (B) 3 tens + 6 ones

   (C) 3 tens + 60 ones   (D) None of these

43. Which of the following shows the largest number?

   (A) 72   (B) 27   (C) 42   (D) 09

44. 8 tens = _____

   (A) 88   (B) 80   (C) 08   (D) None of these.

45. 3 tens 4 ones

   (A) 43   (B) 30   (C) 34   (D) 04

46. 2 tens = _____

   (A) 02   (B) 22   (C) 21   (D) 20

47. 6 tens 3 ones

   (A) 36   (B) 63   (C) 60   (D) None of these.

48. 7 ones 2 tens

   (A) 72   (B) 27   (C) 70   (D) 20

49. Which number comes between 89 and 91?

   (A) 99   (B) 94   (C) 90   (D) 88

50. 7 + 3 tens = _____

   (a) 73   (b) 37   (c) 30   (d) 70

❐❐❐

ANSWERSHEET

1. Ⓐ Ⓑ Ⓒ Ⓓ	2. Ⓐ Ⓑ Ⓒ Ⓓ	3. Ⓐ Ⓑ Ⓒ Ⓓ	4. Ⓐ Ⓑ Ⓒ Ⓓ
5. Ⓐ Ⓑ Ⓒ Ⓓ	6. Ⓐ Ⓑ Ⓒ Ⓓ	7. Ⓐ Ⓑ Ⓒ Ⓓ	8. Ⓐ Ⓑ Ⓒ Ⓓ
9. Ⓐ Ⓑ Ⓒ Ⓓ	10. Ⓐ Ⓑ Ⓒ Ⓓ	11. Ⓐ Ⓑ Ⓒ Ⓓ	12. Ⓐ Ⓑ Ⓒ Ⓓ
13. Ⓐ Ⓑ Ⓒ Ⓓ	14. Ⓐ Ⓑ Ⓒ Ⓓ	15. Ⓐ Ⓑ Ⓒ Ⓓ	16. Ⓐ Ⓑ Ⓒ Ⓓ
17. Ⓐ Ⓑ Ⓒ Ⓓ	18. Ⓐ Ⓑ Ⓒ Ⓓ	19. Ⓐ Ⓑ Ⓒ Ⓓ	20. Ⓐ Ⓑ Ⓒ Ⓓ
21. Ⓐ Ⓑ Ⓒ Ⓓ	22. Ⓐ Ⓑ Ⓒ Ⓓ	23. Ⓐ Ⓑ Ⓒ Ⓓ	24. Ⓐ Ⓑ Ⓒ Ⓓ
25. Ⓐ Ⓑ Ⓒ Ⓓ	26. Ⓐ Ⓑ Ⓒ Ⓓ	27. Ⓐ Ⓑ Ⓒ Ⓓ	28. Ⓐ Ⓑ Ⓒ Ⓓ
29. Ⓐ Ⓑ Ⓒ Ⓓ	30. Ⓐ Ⓑ Ⓒ Ⓓ	31. Ⓐ Ⓑ Ⓒ Ⓓ	32. Ⓐ Ⓑ Ⓒ Ⓓ
33. Ⓐ Ⓑ Ⓒ Ⓓ	34. Ⓐ Ⓑ Ⓒ Ⓓ	35. Ⓐ Ⓑ Ⓒ Ⓓ	36. Ⓐ Ⓑ Ⓒ Ⓓ
37. Ⓐ Ⓑ Ⓒ Ⓓ	38. Ⓐ Ⓑ Ⓒ Ⓓ	39. Ⓐ Ⓑ Ⓒ Ⓓ	40. Ⓐ Ⓑ Ⓒ Ⓓ
41. Ⓐ Ⓑ Ⓒ Ⓓ	42. Ⓐ Ⓑ Ⓒ Ⓓ	43. Ⓐ Ⓑ Ⓒ Ⓓ	44. Ⓐ Ⓑ Ⓒ Ⓓ
45. Ⓐ Ⓑ Ⓒ Ⓓ	46. Ⓐ Ⓑ Ⓒ Ⓓ	47. Ⓐ Ⓑ Ⓒ Ⓓ	48. Ⓐ Ⓑ Ⓒ Ⓓ
49. Ⓐ Ⓑ Ⓒ Ⓓ	50. Ⓐ Ⓑ Ⓒ Ⓓ	51. Ⓐ Ⓑ Ⓒ Ⓓ	52. Ⓐ Ⓑ Ⓒ Ⓓ
53. Ⓐ Ⓑ Ⓒ Ⓓ	54. Ⓐ Ⓑ Ⓒ Ⓓ	55. Ⓐ Ⓑ Ⓒ Ⓓ	56. Ⓐ Ⓑ Ⓒ Ⓓ
57. Ⓐ Ⓑ Ⓒ Ⓓ	58. Ⓐ Ⓑ Ⓒ Ⓓ	59. Ⓐ Ⓑ Ⓒ Ⓓ	60. Ⓐ Ⓑ Ⓒ Ⓓ
61. Ⓐ Ⓑ Ⓒ Ⓓ	62. Ⓐ Ⓑ Ⓒ Ⓓ	63. Ⓐ Ⓑ Ⓒ Ⓓ	64. Ⓐ Ⓑ Ⓒ Ⓓ
65. Ⓐ Ⓑ Ⓒ Ⓓ	66. Ⓐ Ⓑ Ⓒ Ⓓ	67. Ⓐ Ⓑ Ⓒ Ⓓ	68. Ⓐ Ⓑ Ⓒ Ⓓ
69. Ⓐ Ⓑ Ⓒ Ⓓ	70. Ⓐ Ⓑ Ⓒ Ⓓ	71. Ⓐ Ⓑ Ⓒ Ⓓ	72. Ⓐ Ⓑ Ⓒ Ⓓ
73. Ⓐ Ⓑ Ⓒ Ⓓ	74. Ⓐ Ⓑ Ⓒ Ⓓ	75. Ⓐ Ⓑ Ⓒ Ⓓ	76. Ⓐ Ⓑ Ⓒ Ⓓ
77. Ⓐ Ⓑ Ⓒ Ⓓ	78. Ⓐ Ⓑ Ⓒ Ⓓ	79. Ⓐ Ⓑ Ⓒ Ⓓ	80. Ⓐ Ⓑ Ⓒ Ⓓ
81. Ⓐ Ⓑ Ⓒ Ⓓ	82. Ⓐ Ⓑ Ⓒ Ⓓ	83. Ⓐ Ⓑ Ⓒ Ⓓ	84. Ⓐ Ⓑ Ⓒ Ⓓ
85. Ⓐ Ⓑ Ⓒ Ⓓ	86. Ⓐ Ⓑ Ⓒ Ⓓ	87. Ⓐ Ⓑ Ⓒ Ⓓ	88. Ⓐ Ⓑ Ⓒ Ⓓ
89. Ⓐ Ⓑ Ⓒ Ⓓ	90. Ⓐ Ⓑ Ⓒ Ⓓ	91. Ⓐ Ⓑ Ⓒ Ⓓ	92. Ⓐ Ⓑ Ⓒ Ⓓ
93. Ⓐ Ⓑ Ⓒ Ⓓ	94. Ⓐ Ⓑ Ⓒ Ⓓ	95. Ⓐ Ⓑ Ⓒ Ⓓ	96. Ⓐ Ⓑ Ⓒ Ⓓ
97. Ⓐ Ⓑ Ⓒ Ⓓ	98. Ⓐ Ⓑ Ⓒ Ⓓ	99. Ⓐ Ⓑ Ⓒ Ⓓ	100. Ⓐ Ⓑ Ⓒ Ⓓ

Chapter 2
ADDITION

Topics: - Addition without carry over and with carryover, Addition on number line, addition on abacus, addition word problems.

Important points

ADDITION RULE: Numbers can be added in any order. Answer will not change by changing the order of the numbers.

When you add 0 to any number, answer is that same number.

Key words for addition are total, sum, altogether, in all.

Choose the Correct Answer

1.   6 tens + 2 tens = _____

     (A) 66 tens   (B) 80 tens   (C) 8 tens   (D) 10 tens

2. $\boxed{90}$ + $\boxed{3}$ = _____

     (A) 39   (B) 93   (C) 90   (D) 30

3.   If I add this number to 40, I will get 40. What am I adding?

         40 + _____ = 40

     (A) 40   (B) 1   (C) 0   (D) 44

4.   3 more than 34 + 12 is

     (A) 46   (B) 43   (C) 49   (D) None of these.

5.   Which is more?

         40 + 3   40 + 9   50 + 9   40 + 8

     (A) 40 + 3   (B) 40 + 9   (C) 50 + 9   (D) 40 + 8

6. If I add this number to 81, I will get 82. What am I adding?

   81 + ____ = 82

   (A) 0   (B) 80   (C) 81   (D) 1

7. 5 tens + 4 tens = ____

   (A) 90 tens   (B) 9 tens   (C) 99 tens   (D) 44 ones

8. 36 + 14 =

   (A) 40   (B) 50   (C) 22   (D) None of these

9. 8 more than 78 is

   (A) 70   (B) 86   (C) 77   (D) None of these

10. 18 more than 42 + 33 is _____

    (A) 75   (B) 88   (C) 80   (D) None of these.

11.   70

    +   20
    ―――――

    (A) 50   (B) 90   (C) 30   (D) None of these.

12. 12 + 5 is shown by which abacus?

(A)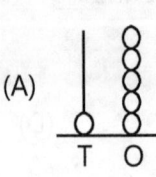

(B)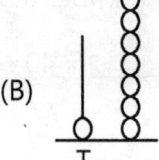

(C)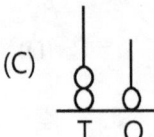

(D)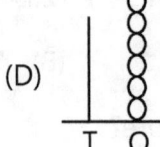

13. Which two numbers when added will give 9?

    (A) 3 + 3   (B) 6 + 3   (C) 9 + 3   (D) 2 + 4

14. Bhoomi has 46 pencils, she buys another 4 pencils. How many pencils does she have altogether?

    (A) 42   (B) 40   (C) 50   (D) 44

15. In a basket there are 6 apples, 8 mangoes, and 15 bananas. How many fruits are there in the basket?

    (A) 21   (B) 23   (C) 29   (D) 19

16. Complete the number bond.

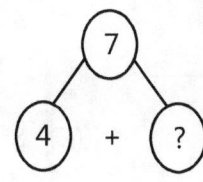

    (A) 4   (B) 3   (C) 2   (D) 1

17. A girl jumps 2 steps from 0 and then 3 steps. Where will she reach?

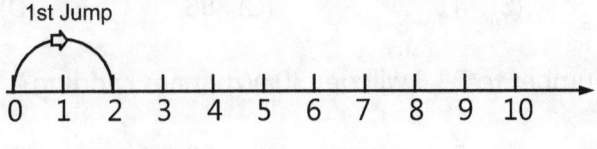

    (A) 1   (B) 5   (C) 6   (D) 9

18. Which 2 numbers when added will give 12?

    (A) 6 + 4   (B) 4 + 3   (C) 9 + 2   (D) 6 + 6

19. Ronit has 83 toys. He buys another 7 toys. How many toys does he have altogether?

    (A) 76   (B) 90   (C) 88   (D) 97

20. In a jungle there are 18 elephants, 24 rabbits and 7 tigers. How many animals are there in the jungle?

    (A) 49   (B) 31   (C) 25   (D) 42

21. Complete the number bond.

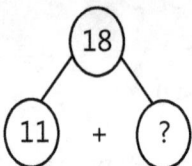

   (A) 8   (B) 7   (C) 17   (D) None of these

22. Kalu has 2 pencils

    Ved has 4 pencils

    Total no. of pencils = _____

    (A) 1   (B) 6   (C) 8   (D) 3

23. There are 14 boys and 27 girls in a class. How many children are there in all
    in the class?

    (A) 40   (B) 41   (C) 56   (D) 13

24. If I add this number to 23, I will get 30. What am I adding?

    (A) 7   (B) 53   (C) 60   (D) 46

25. I have 9 pens, Raja gave me 6 more. Tina gave me 4 more. How many pens
    do I have altogether?

    (A) 15   (B) 19   (C) 13   (D) None of these.

26. How many balls are there in all?

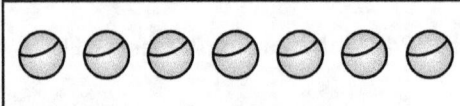   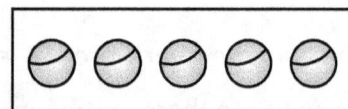

    (A) 7 + 5   (B) 5 + 7   (C) Both A & B   (D) 7 + 6

27.

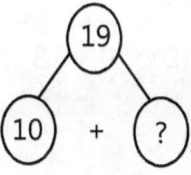

    (A) 35 + 24 = 59   (B) 53 + 24 = 77

    (C) 53 + 42 = 95   (D) None of these.

28. Dev has 48 books. He buys another 12 books. How many books does he have altogether?

    (A) 36   (B) 60   (C) 52   (D) None of these.

29.

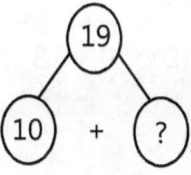

    (A) 1   (B) 9   (C) 2   (D) 6

30. Which two numbers when added will give 46?

    (A) 20 + 16   (B) 26 + 40   (C) 26 + 20   (D) None of these.

31. A girl jumps 4 steps from 0 and then 3 steps. Where will she reach?

    1st Jump

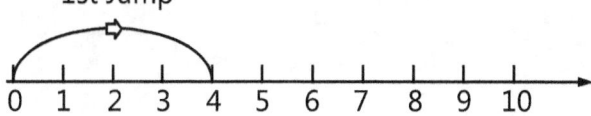

    (A) 3rd Point   (B) 7th Point   (C) 5th Point   (D) None of these.

32. I have 9 erasers. John gave me 6 more. Tom gave me 5 more. How many erasers I have?

    (A) 9 + 6 + 5   (B) 6 + 9 + 5   (C) Both A & B   (D) 9 + 4 + 5

33.  62 + 57 = _____

    (A) 119   (B) 15   (C) 91   (D) None of these

34. 8 more than 17 + 41 is

    (A) 58   (B) 25   (C) 66   (D) None of these.

35. 32 + 46 = _____

    (A) 32 + 46   (B) 42 + 36   (C) 46 + 32   (D) Both A & C

36. Which is more?

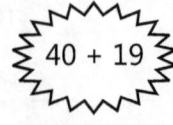 

    60 + 7   30 + 14   40 + 19   70 + 18

    (A) 60 + 7   (B) 30 + 14   (C) 40 + 19   (D) 70 + 18

37.

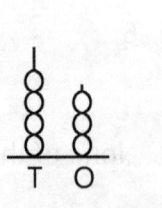 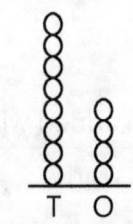 Shows

    (A) 41 + 43 = 84   (B) 44 + 43 = 87

    (C) 34 + 14 = 48   (D) None of these

38. I have 28 dolls. Mona has 49 dolls. Total number of dolls = _____

    (A) 67   (B) 71   (C) 76   (D) 77

39. 6 more than 10 is

    (A) 10 + 6   (B) 16 + 6   (C) 10 + 16   (D) None of these

40. 8 more than 12 is represented as

(A) 12 + 8   (B) 18 + 2   (C) 18 + 12   (D) None of these

41. 5 more than 11 is represented by which number line?

(A)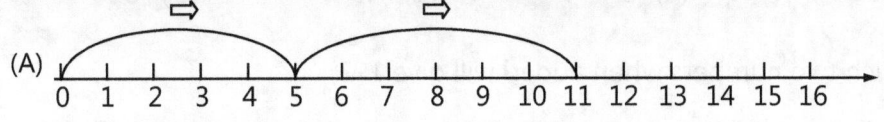

(B)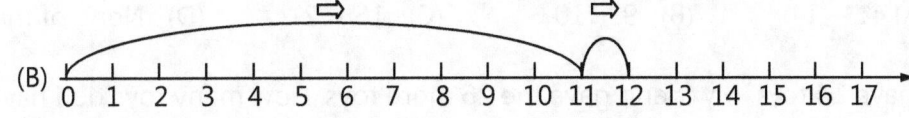

(C)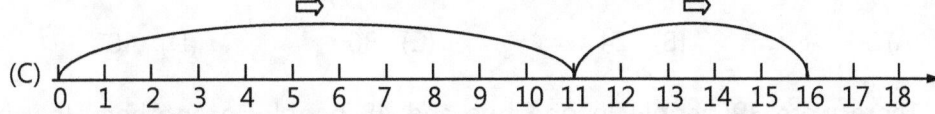

(D) None of these

42. 3 tens + 2 tens = _____

(A) 32 tens   (B) 50 tens   (C) 30 tens   (D) 5 tens

43. 6 tens + 1 tens = _____

(A) 60 tens   (B) 70 tens   (C) 7 tens   (D) 61 tens

44. 5 tens + 2 tens = _____

(A) 50 + 20 = 70   (B) 5 + 20 = 25   (C) 50 + 2 = 52   (D) None of these.

45. 4 more than 8 is represented by which number line.

(A)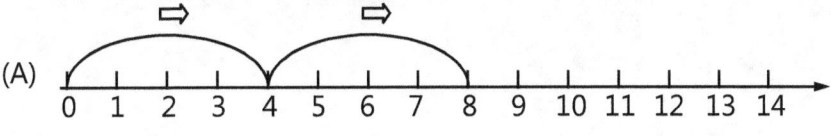

(B)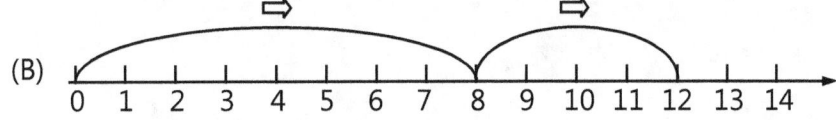

(C)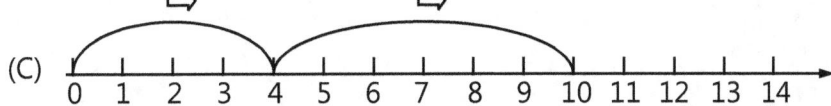

(D) None of these

46. There are 42 boys and 39 girls in a class. How many children are there in the class?

(A) 02   (B) 94   (C) 49   (D) 81

47. Which two numbers when added will give 19?

(A) 41 + 14   (B) 9 + 10   (C) 16 + 21   (D) None of these

48. I have 14 toys. My friend gave me 26 more toys. How many toys do I have?

(A) 30   (B) 24   (C) 36   (D) 40

49. There were 39 people in one bus and 48 people in another. How many people were there in two buses?

(A) 38+49   (B) 39 + 48   (C) 48 + 39   (D) Both B and C

50. 29 + 30 = ____

(A) 50   (B) 59   (C) 1   (D) None of these

❏❏❏

ANSWERSHEET

1.	Ⓐ Ⓑ Ⓒ Ⓓ	2.	Ⓐ Ⓑ Ⓒ Ⓓ	3.	Ⓐ Ⓑ Ⓒ Ⓓ	4.	Ⓐ Ⓑ Ⓒ Ⓓ
5.	Ⓐ Ⓑ Ⓒ Ⓓ	6.	Ⓐ Ⓑ Ⓒ Ⓓ	7.	Ⓐ Ⓑ Ⓒ Ⓓ	8.	Ⓐ Ⓑ Ⓒ Ⓓ
9.	Ⓐ Ⓑ Ⓒ Ⓓ	10.	Ⓐ Ⓑ Ⓒ Ⓓ	11.	Ⓐ Ⓑ Ⓒ Ⓓ	12.	Ⓐ Ⓑ Ⓒ Ⓓ
13.	Ⓐ Ⓑ Ⓒ Ⓓ	14.	Ⓐ Ⓑ Ⓒ Ⓓ	15.	Ⓐ Ⓑ Ⓒ Ⓓ	16.	Ⓐ Ⓑ Ⓒ Ⓓ
17.	Ⓐ Ⓑ Ⓒ Ⓓ	18.	Ⓐ Ⓑ Ⓒ Ⓓ	19.	Ⓐ Ⓑ Ⓒ Ⓓ	20.	Ⓐ Ⓑ Ⓒ Ⓓ
21.	Ⓐ Ⓑ Ⓒ Ⓓ	22.	Ⓐ Ⓑ Ⓒ Ⓓ	23.	Ⓐ Ⓑ Ⓒ Ⓓ	24.	Ⓐ Ⓑ Ⓒ Ⓓ
25.	Ⓐ Ⓑ Ⓒ Ⓓ	26.	Ⓐ Ⓑ Ⓒ Ⓓ	27.	Ⓐ Ⓑ Ⓒ Ⓓ	28.	Ⓐ Ⓑ Ⓒ Ⓓ
29.	Ⓐ Ⓑ Ⓒ Ⓓ	30.	Ⓐ Ⓑ Ⓒ Ⓓ	31.	Ⓐ Ⓑ Ⓒ Ⓓ	32.	Ⓐ Ⓑ Ⓒ Ⓓ
33.	Ⓐ Ⓑ Ⓒ Ⓓ	34.	Ⓐ Ⓑ Ⓒ Ⓓ	35.	Ⓐ Ⓑ Ⓒ Ⓓ	36.	Ⓐ Ⓑ Ⓒ Ⓓ
37.	Ⓐ Ⓑ Ⓒ Ⓓ	38.	Ⓐ Ⓑ Ⓒ Ⓓ	39.	Ⓐ Ⓑ Ⓒ Ⓓ	40.	Ⓐ Ⓑ Ⓒ Ⓓ
41.	Ⓐ Ⓑ Ⓒ Ⓓ	42.	Ⓐ Ⓑ Ⓒ Ⓓ	43.	Ⓐ Ⓑ Ⓒ Ⓓ	44.	Ⓐ Ⓑ Ⓒ Ⓓ
45.	Ⓐ Ⓑ Ⓒ Ⓓ	46.	Ⓐ Ⓑ Ⓒ Ⓓ	47.	Ⓐ Ⓑ Ⓒ Ⓓ	48.	Ⓐ Ⓑ Ⓒ Ⓓ
49.	Ⓐ Ⓑ Ⓒ Ⓓ	50.	Ⓐ Ⓑ Ⓒ Ⓓ	51.	Ⓐ Ⓑ Ⓒ Ⓓ	52.	Ⓐ Ⓑ Ⓒ Ⓓ
53.	Ⓐ Ⓑ Ⓒ Ⓓ	54.	Ⓐ Ⓑ Ⓒ Ⓓ	55.	Ⓐ Ⓑ Ⓒ Ⓓ	56.	Ⓐ Ⓑ Ⓒ Ⓓ
57.	Ⓐ Ⓑ Ⓒ Ⓓ	58.	Ⓐ Ⓑ Ⓒ Ⓓ	59.	Ⓐ Ⓑ Ⓒ Ⓓ	60.	Ⓐ Ⓑ Ⓒ Ⓓ
61.	Ⓐ Ⓑ Ⓒ Ⓓ	62.	Ⓐ Ⓑ Ⓒ Ⓓ	63.	Ⓐ Ⓑ Ⓒ Ⓓ	64.	Ⓐ Ⓑ Ⓒ Ⓓ
65.	Ⓐ Ⓑ Ⓒ Ⓓ	66.	Ⓐ Ⓑ Ⓒ Ⓓ	67.	Ⓐ Ⓑ Ⓒ Ⓓ	68.	Ⓐ Ⓑ Ⓒ Ⓓ
69.	Ⓐ Ⓑ Ⓒ Ⓓ	70.	Ⓐ Ⓑ Ⓒ Ⓓ	71.	Ⓐ Ⓑ Ⓒ Ⓓ	72.	Ⓐ Ⓑ Ⓒ Ⓓ
73.	Ⓐ Ⓑ Ⓒ Ⓓ	74.	Ⓐ Ⓑ Ⓒ Ⓓ	75.	Ⓐ Ⓑ Ⓒ Ⓓ	76.	Ⓐ Ⓑ Ⓒ Ⓓ
77.	Ⓐ Ⓑ Ⓒ Ⓓ	78.	Ⓐ Ⓑ Ⓒ Ⓓ	79.	Ⓐ Ⓑ Ⓒ Ⓓ	80.	Ⓐ Ⓑ Ⓒ Ⓓ
81.	Ⓐ Ⓑ Ⓒ Ⓓ	82.	Ⓐ Ⓑ Ⓒ Ⓓ	83.	Ⓐ Ⓑ Ⓒ Ⓓ	84.	Ⓐ Ⓑ Ⓒ Ⓓ
85.	Ⓐ Ⓑ Ⓒ Ⓓ	86.	Ⓐ Ⓑ Ⓒ Ⓓ	87.	Ⓐ Ⓑ Ⓒ Ⓓ	88.	Ⓐ Ⓑ Ⓒ Ⓓ
89.	Ⓐ Ⓑ Ⓒ Ⓓ	90.	Ⓐ Ⓑ Ⓒ Ⓓ	91.	Ⓐ Ⓑ Ⓒ Ⓓ	92.	Ⓐ Ⓑ Ⓒ Ⓓ
93.	Ⓐ Ⓑ Ⓒ Ⓓ	94.	Ⓐ Ⓑ Ⓒ Ⓓ	95.	Ⓐ Ⓑ Ⓒ Ⓓ	96.	Ⓐ Ⓑ Ⓒ Ⓓ
97.	Ⓐ Ⓑ Ⓒ Ⓓ	98.	Ⓐ Ⓑ Ⓒ Ⓓ	99.	Ⓐ Ⓑ Ⓒ Ⓓ	100.	Ⓐ Ⓑ Ⓒ Ⓓ

Chapter 3
SUBTRACTION

Topics: Subtraction without borrowing and with borrowing, subtraction on number line, subtraction on abacus, subtraction word problems.

Important Points

When you remove something from a collection you can say 'take away', we use '–' sign.

Subtraction rule: We can't subtract a greater number from a smaller number.

When something becomes less from the total collection we subtract.

Key words for subtraction: difference, takeaway, how many more left, how many less, how many left, went away.

Choose the Correct Answer

1. There are 10 balls in a basket. Heena took away 2 balls. How many balls are left in the basket?

   (A) 12   (B) 8   (C) 20   (D) None of these.

2. There are 15 butterflies. 3 butterflies flew away. How many butterflies are left?

   (A) 15 – 3 = 12   (B) 3 – 15 = 12   (C) 13 – 5 = 8   (D) None of these.

3. Raj ate 7 chocolates from a packet of 19 chocolates. How many are left?

   (A) 17 – 9 = 12   (B) 19 – 7 = 12   (C) 7 – 19 = 12   (D) None of these.

4. Which of the following is the other way of 8 less than 19.

   (A) 19 – 8 = 11   (B) 19 – 11 = 8   (C) 11 – 8 = 2   (D) 11 + 8 = 9

5. $\bigcirc$ = 20 and $\bigcirc$ = 10, then which of the following is correct?

   (A) $\bigcirc - \bigcirc = \bigcirc\bigcirc$ (B) $\bigcirc - \bigcirc = \bigcirc$

   (C) $\bigcirc - \bigcirc = \bigcirc$ (D) $\bigcirc - \bigcirc = \bigcirc\bigcirc$

6. Take away 3 from 9 to give

   (A) 4 (B) 6 (C) 3 (D) 12

7. $\boxed{}$ = 28, $\boxed{}$ = 14, then which of the following is correct?

   (A) $\boxed{} - \boxed{} = \boxed{}$ (B) $\boxed{} - \boxed{} = \boxed{}$

   (C) $\boxed{} - \boxed{} = \boxed{}\boxed{}$ (D) $\boxed{} - \boxed{} = \boxed{}$

8. Which of the following is the other way of 9 less than 36?

   (A) 36 – 9 = 27 (B) 36 – 27 = 9 (C) 36 + 9 = 45 (D) None of these.

9. 93 – 27 =

   (A) 66 (B) 74 (C) 64 (D) None of these

10. There are 32 balloons. 14 balloons bursted. How many balloons are left?

    (A) 18 (B) 46 (C) 34 (D) None of these.

11. Which is same as 14 – 9 =?

    (A) 15 – 3 (B) 10 – 5 (C) 14 – 4 (D) None of these

12. How many balls should be crossed 'X' to show 12 – 5 = 7?

    (A) 12 (B) 5 (C) 7 (D) None of these

13. Rishu has 6 icecreams

    She gave 4 to her sister Anushka. How many are left?

    (A) 6 – 2 = 4 (B) 6 – 4 = 2 (C) 6 + 4 = 10 (D) None of these.

14. 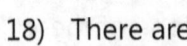 -  =

   (A) 9   (B) 2   (C) 11   (D) 7

15. 8 tens 4 ones – 3 tens 2 ones =

   (A) 42   (B) 67   (C) 52   (D) None of these.

16. Riya has 14 pens. She gave 6 pens to Mona. How many pens are left?

   (A) 14 – 6 = 8   (B) 16 – 4 = 12   (C) 14 – 8 = 6   (D) None of these

17. There are 22 bugs in the garden 14 bugs went away. How many are left?

   (A) 36   (B) 24   (C) 42   (D) 8

18) There are  in the freezer.

melted. How many are left?

   (A) 10   (B) 2   (C) 12   (D) None of these.

19. Which is same as $\boxed{30}$ – $\boxed{14}$

   (A) $\boxed{36}$ – $\boxed{14}$ (B) $\boxed{24}$ – $\boxed{10}$ (C) $\boxed{40}$ – $\boxed{30}$ (D) $\boxed{40}$ – $\boxed{24}$

20.

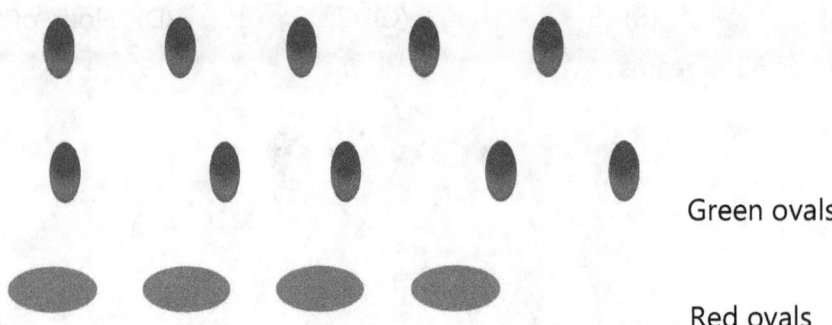

Green ovals

Red ovals

How many red ovals are needed to make equal to green ovals?

   (A) 14   (B) 6   (C) 4   (D) None of these.

21. 9 - 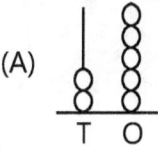   =

     (A) 5   (B) 4   (C) 14   (D) None of these

22. 96 – 29

     (A) 67   (B) 99   (C) 62   (D) None of these

23. 8 tens 9 ones – 3 tens 9 ones =

     (A) 80 – 9 = 71   (B) 89 – 9 = 80   (C) 89 – 39 = 50 (D) None of these

24.

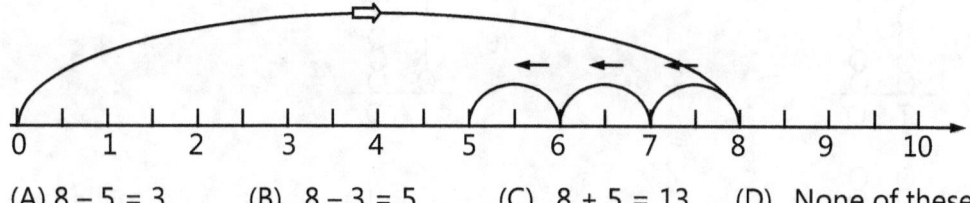

     (A) 8 – 5 = 3   (B) 8 – 3 = 5   (C) 8 + 5 = 13   (D) None of these.

25. A shopkeeper sold 28 dolls on Wednesday. He sold 4 dolls less on Thursday.
     How many did he sell on Thursday.

     (A) 32   (B) 24   (C) 20   (D) None of these.

26. Which abacus shows 27 – 14 = 13?

     (A)   (B)

     (C)   (D)

27. Take away 12 from 48 to give

     (A) 60   (B) 36   (C) 40   (D) 26

28. Which is least?

$$\boxed{30 - 6} \quad \boxed{32 - 18} \quad \boxed{26 - 10} \quad \boxed{48 - 13}$$

(A) 30 – 6   (B) 32 – 18   (C) 26 – 10   (D) 48 – 13

29. I have 50 sweets, Bhoomi ate 12 sweets. How many sweets are left?

(A) 50 – 12 = 38   (B) 50 – 38 = 12

(C) 50 + 38 = 88   (D) None of these.

30. 63 – 13 shown by which abacus?

31. 8 tens – 3 tens = _____

(A) 80 tens   (B) 50 tens   (C) 5 tens   (D) 30 tens

32. 9 tens – 6 tens = _____

(A) 69 tens   (B) 52 tens   (C) 17 tens   (D) None of these

33. 7 tens 4 ones – 3 tens 3 ones = _____

(A) 4 tens 1 ones   (B) 4 tens 6 ones

(C) 8 tens 9 ones   (D) 3 tens 1 ones

34.

What does this show you?

(A) 9 – 7= 2   (B) 9 – 2 = 7   (C) 9 - 3 = 6   (D) None of these.

35. $12 -$ 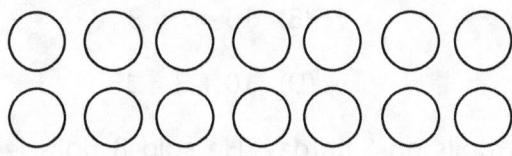 $=$

(A) 7   (B) 5   (C) 17   (D) None of these.

36.   How many circles should be crossed 'X' to show $14 - 6 = 8$

(A) 14   (B) 6   (C) 8   (D) 5

37.   Which of the following is the other way of 19 less than 32?

(A) $32 - 19 = 13$ (B) $32 - 13 = 19$

(C) $19 - 5 = 14$ (D) $32 + 19 = 51$

38.   ▯ $= 20$, ☐ $= 10$, then which of the following is correct?

(A) ▯ – ☐ = ☐   (B) ▯ – ☐ = ☐ ☐

(C) ▯ – ☐ = ▯   (D) ▯ – ☐ = ☐ ▯

39.   Which abacus shows $32 - 10 = 22$?

(A)   (B)
    T   O   T   O

(C)   (D)
    T   O   T   O

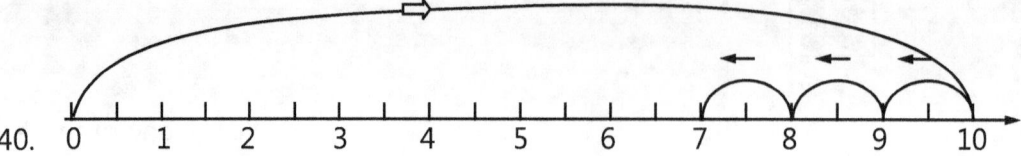

40. Shows _____

(A) 10 – 3 = 7   (B) 10 – 7 = 3

(C) 10 – 9 = 1   (D) 10 + 3 = 13

41. A shopkeeper sold 48 dolls on Saturday. He sold 8 dolls less on Sunday. How many dolls are sold on Sunday?

(A) 48 – 8 = 40   (B) 48 + 8 = 35

(C) 48 – 40 = 8   (D) 48 – 2 = 46

42. A shopkeeper sold 39 pencils in January month. He sold 4 pencils less in February. How many pencils were sold in February?

(A) 39 + 4 = 43   (B) 39 - 4 = 35   (C) 39 – 35 = 4   (D) 39 – 30 = 9

43.

 Blue balls

Brown balls

How many brown balls are needed to make equal to blue balls?

(A) 3   (B) 7   (C) 4   (D) 8

44. Take away 6 from 28 to give

(A) 22   (B) 34   (C) 20   (D) 30

45. Take away 19 from 49 to give

(A) 68   (B) 30   (C) 54   (D) 36

46. There are 49 balloons. 32 are blown away. How many are left?

(A) 17   (B) 81   (C) 63   (D) 44

47. 🦃🦃🦃🦃🦃 – 🦃🦃🦃

(A) 5   (B) 3   (C) 8   (D) 2

48. Kuhu has 57 dolls. She gave 36 dolls to her sister. How many dolls are left with Kuhu?

(A) 21   (B) 92   (C) 34   (D) None of these

49. Raju eats 13 biscuits from a packet of 20 biscuits. How many are left?

(A) 33   (B) 7   (C) 52   (D) 24

50. 9 tens – 7 tens = _____

(A) 69 tens   (B) 2 tens   (C) 17 tens   (D) None of these

❑❑❑

ANSWERSHEET

1.	Ⓐ Ⓑ Ⓒ Ⓓ	2.	Ⓐ Ⓑ Ⓒ Ⓓ	3.	Ⓐ Ⓑ Ⓒ Ⓓ	4.	Ⓐ Ⓑ Ⓒ Ⓓ
5.	Ⓐ Ⓑ Ⓒ Ⓓ	6.	Ⓐ Ⓑ Ⓒ Ⓓ	7.	Ⓐ Ⓑ Ⓒ Ⓓ	8.	Ⓐ Ⓑ Ⓒ Ⓓ
9.	Ⓐ Ⓑ Ⓒ Ⓓ	10.	Ⓐ Ⓑ Ⓒ Ⓓ	11.	Ⓐ Ⓑ Ⓒ Ⓓ	12.	Ⓐ Ⓑ Ⓒ Ⓓ
13.	Ⓐ Ⓑ Ⓒ Ⓓ	14.	Ⓐ Ⓑ Ⓒ Ⓓ	15.	Ⓐ Ⓑ Ⓒ Ⓓ	16.	Ⓐ Ⓑ Ⓒ Ⓓ
17.	Ⓐ Ⓑ Ⓒ Ⓓ	18.	Ⓐ Ⓑ Ⓒ Ⓓ	19.	Ⓐ Ⓑ Ⓒ Ⓓ	20.	Ⓐ Ⓑ Ⓒ Ⓓ
21.	Ⓐ Ⓑ Ⓒ Ⓓ	22.	Ⓐ Ⓑ Ⓒ Ⓓ	23.	Ⓐ Ⓑ Ⓒ Ⓓ	24.	Ⓐ Ⓑ Ⓒ Ⓓ
25.	Ⓐ Ⓑ Ⓒ Ⓓ	26.	Ⓐ Ⓑ Ⓒ Ⓓ	27.	Ⓐ Ⓑ Ⓒ Ⓓ	28.	Ⓐ Ⓑ Ⓒ Ⓓ
29.	Ⓐ Ⓑ Ⓒ Ⓓ	30.	Ⓐ Ⓑ Ⓒ Ⓓ	31.	Ⓐ Ⓑ Ⓒ Ⓓ	32.	Ⓐ Ⓑ Ⓒ Ⓓ
33.	Ⓐ Ⓑ Ⓒ Ⓓ	34.	Ⓐ Ⓑ Ⓒ Ⓓ	35.	Ⓐ Ⓑ Ⓒ Ⓓ	36.	Ⓐ Ⓑ Ⓒ Ⓓ
37.	Ⓐ Ⓑ Ⓒ Ⓓ	38.	Ⓐ Ⓑ Ⓒ Ⓓ	39.	Ⓐ Ⓑ Ⓒ Ⓓ	40.	Ⓐ Ⓑ Ⓒ Ⓓ
41.	Ⓐ Ⓑ Ⓒ Ⓓ	42.	Ⓐ Ⓑ Ⓒ Ⓓ	43.	Ⓐ Ⓑ Ⓒ Ⓓ	44.	Ⓐ Ⓑ Ⓒ Ⓓ
45.	Ⓐ Ⓑ Ⓒ Ⓓ	46.	Ⓐ Ⓑ Ⓒ Ⓓ	47.	Ⓐ Ⓑ Ⓒ Ⓓ	48.	Ⓐ Ⓑ Ⓒ Ⓓ
49.	Ⓐ Ⓑ Ⓒ Ⓓ	50.	Ⓐ Ⓑ Ⓒ Ⓓ	51.	Ⓐ Ⓑ Ⓒ Ⓓ	52.	Ⓐ Ⓑ Ⓒ Ⓓ
53.	Ⓐ Ⓑ Ⓒ Ⓓ	54.	Ⓐ Ⓑ Ⓒ Ⓓ	55.	Ⓐ Ⓑ Ⓒ Ⓓ	56.	Ⓐ Ⓑ Ⓒ Ⓓ
57.	Ⓐ Ⓑ Ⓒ Ⓓ	58.	Ⓐ Ⓑ Ⓒ Ⓓ	59.	Ⓐ Ⓑ Ⓒ Ⓓ	60.	Ⓐ Ⓑ Ⓒ Ⓓ
61.	Ⓐ Ⓑ Ⓒ Ⓓ	62.	Ⓐ Ⓑ Ⓒ Ⓓ	63.	Ⓐ Ⓑ Ⓒ Ⓓ	64.	Ⓐ Ⓑ Ⓒ Ⓓ
65.	Ⓐ Ⓑ Ⓒ Ⓓ	66.	Ⓐ Ⓑ Ⓒ Ⓓ	67.	Ⓐ Ⓑ Ⓒ Ⓓ	68.	Ⓐ Ⓑ Ⓒ Ⓓ
69.	Ⓐ Ⓑ Ⓒ Ⓓ	70.	Ⓐ Ⓑ Ⓒ Ⓓ	71.	Ⓐ Ⓑ Ⓒ Ⓓ	72.	Ⓐ Ⓑ Ⓒ Ⓓ
73.	Ⓐ Ⓑ Ⓒ Ⓓ	74.	Ⓐ Ⓑ Ⓒ Ⓓ	75.	Ⓐ Ⓑ Ⓒ Ⓓ	76.	Ⓐ Ⓑ Ⓒ Ⓓ
77.	Ⓐ Ⓑ Ⓒ Ⓓ	78.	Ⓐ Ⓑ Ⓒ Ⓓ	79.	Ⓐ Ⓑ Ⓒ Ⓓ	80.	Ⓐ Ⓑ Ⓒ Ⓓ
81.	Ⓐ Ⓑ Ⓒ Ⓓ	82.	Ⓐ Ⓑ Ⓒ Ⓓ	83.	Ⓐ Ⓑ Ⓒ Ⓓ	84.	Ⓐ Ⓑ Ⓒ Ⓓ
85.	Ⓐ Ⓑ Ⓒ Ⓓ	86.	Ⓐ Ⓑ Ⓒ Ⓓ	87.	Ⓐ Ⓑ Ⓒ Ⓓ	88.	Ⓐ Ⓑ Ⓒ Ⓓ
89.	Ⓐ Ⓑ Ⓒ Ⓓ	90.	Ⓐ Ⓑ Ⓒ Ⓓ	91.	Ⓐ Ⓑ Ⓒ Ⓓ	92.	Ⓐ Ⓑ Ⓒ Ⓓ
93.	Ⓐ Ⓑ Ⓒ Ⓓ	94.	Ⓐ Ⓑ Ⓒ Ⓓ	95.	Ⓐ Ⓑ Ⓒ Ⓓ	96.	Ⓐ Ⓑ Ⓒ Ⓓ
97.	Ⓐ Ⓑ Ⓒ Ⓓ	98.	Ⓐ Ⓑ Ⓒ Ⓓ	99.	Ⓐ Ⓑ Ⓒ Ⓓ	100.	Ⓐ Ⓑ Ⓒ Ⓓ

Chapter 4
MONEY

Topics: Rupees and paise concept, coins and notes, exchanging money, counting money

Important points

Four 25 paise make 1 Rupee

$$
\begin{array}{r}
25\ p \\
+\ 25\ p \\
+\ 25\ p \\
+\ 25\ p \\
\hline
100\ p = \text{Rupee }1
\end{array}
$$

AND

Two 50 paise coins make 1 rupee.

$$
\begin{array}{r}
50\ p \\
+\ \ \ 50\ p \\
\hline
100\ P = \text{Rupee }1
\end{array}
$$

Choose the Correct Answer

1. ₹ 4 =

(A) ₹2 + ₹2   (B) ₹2 + ₹4

(C) ₹3 + ₹3   (D) 50 P + ₹4

2. How much money is enough to buy this ball?

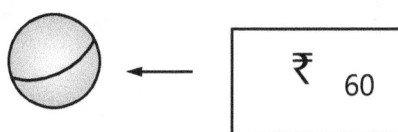 ← ₹ 60

(A) ₹ 20   (B) ₹ 100

(C) ₹ 25   (D) ₹10

3.   How much is the total amount shown here?

(A) ₹ 60   (B) ₹ 65   (C) ₹ 55   (D) ₹ 15

4.   How much is the total amount shown here?

(A) ₹ 30   (B) ₹ 32   (C) ₹ 12   (D) ₹ 22

5.   ₹ 8 =

(A) 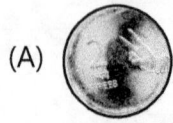 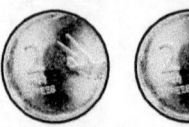    (B)

(C)      (D) None of these

6.   How much money is enough to buy this balloon?

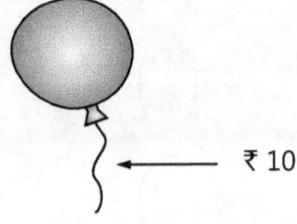

← ₹ 10

(A) ₹ 2   (B) ₹ 5   (C) ₹ 20   (D) ₹ 1

7.   How much money is needed to buy this mango?

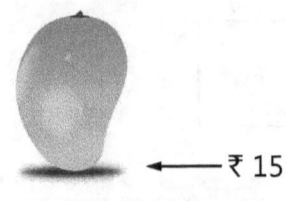

← ₹ 15

(A) ₹ 5   (B) ₹ 15   (C) ₹ 10   (D) ₹ 2

8. If one pencil costs ₹ 10, how much money does Varun need to pay for 2 pencils?

    (A) ₹ 20   (B) ₹ 10   (C) ₹ 2   (D) None of these

9. Rita has ₹ 50, which of the following toys can she buy?

    (A) ₹ 100   (B) ₹ 150   (C) ₹ 30   (D) None of these

10. ₹ 2 = ____

    (A) Four 50 paise coins   (B) Five 50 paise coins

    (C) Four 10 paise coins   (D) Ten 10 paise coins

11. ₹ 3 = ____ paise

    (A) 30   (B) 300   (C) 13   (D) None of these

12. ₹ 5 = ____ paise

    (A) 5   (B) 50   (C) 500   (D) 51

13. ₹ 8 = ____ paise

    (A) 800   (B) 80   (C) 88   (D) 8

14. ₹ 1 = ____ paise

    (A) Two 10 paise coins   (B) Four 20 paise coins

    (C) Two 50 paise coins   (D) Five 25 paise coins

15. ₹ 5 = ____

    (A) Four 50 paise coins   (B) Five 1 rupee coins

    (C) Five 10 paise coins   (D) None of these

16. ₹ 4 = ____

(A) Four 10 paise coins (B) Five 50 rupee coins

(C) Eight 50 paise coins (D) None of these

17. ₹ 7 = ____ paise

(A) 77 (B) 07 (C) 70 (D) 700

18. If one book costs ₹ 5, how much money does Mona needs to pay for 3 books?

(A) 9 (B) 15 (C) 10 (D) 5

19. How much is the total amount shown here?

(A) ₹ 20 (B) ₹ 70 (C) ₹ 170 (D) ₹ 150

20. How much is the amount shown here?

(A) ₹ 25 (B) ₹ 175 (C) ₹ 150 (D) ₹ 185

21. Raju has ₹50. Which of the following can he buy?

(A)  ₹ 30 (C)  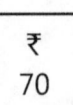 ₹ 70

(B)   ₹ 90 (D)  ₹ 100

22. Mohan has ₹ 80. Which of the following can he buy?

(A) 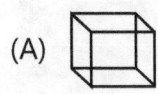 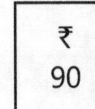 | ₹ 90   (B) 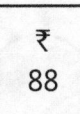 | ₹ 88

(C) 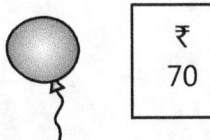 | ₹ 70   (D)   | ₹ 100

23. One ball costs ₹ 10. How many balls can Rahul buy for ₹ 30?

(A) 2   (B) 3   (C) 4   (D) None of these

24. One teddy costs ₹ 10, How many teddies can Raj buy for ₹ 40?

(A) 4   (B) 2   (C) 3   (D) 5

25. Which set shows ₹ 4 ?

(A)

(B)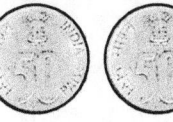

(C)

(D)

26. One toy car costs ₹ 5, How many toy cars can Mehul buy for ₹ 10?

(A) 5   (B) 3   (C) 4   (D) 2

27. Which set shows ₹ 5?

(D) None of these

28. How much money is shown here?

(A) ₹ 50 and 50 p.   (B) ₹ 51 and 50 p.

(C) ₹ 52 and 50 p.   (D) ₹ 50

29. How much money is shown here?

(A) ₹ 22   (B) ₹ 24 and 50 p.

(C) ₹ 20 and 50 p.   (D) None of these.

30. How much money is shown here?

(A) ₹ 73 and 50 p.   (B) ₹ 70 and 50 p.

(C) ₹ 13 and 50 p.   (D) ₹ 73

31. Meena has ₹ 50. She pays for the 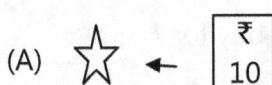 and _____

(A) ☆ ← [₹ 10]   (B) ← [₹ 20]

(C) ← [₹ 40]   (D) None of these

32. Ved pays ₹60 for the △ ← [₹ 20] and _____

(A) 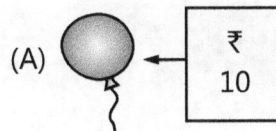 ← [₹ 10]   (B) 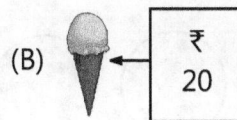 ← [₹ 20]

(C) 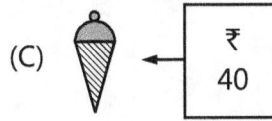 ← [₹ 40]   (D) 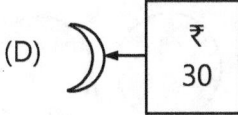 ← [₹ 30]

33. Rita pays ₹ 50 for the ☽ ← ₹ 30 for and _____

(A) ← ₹ 50   (B) ☺ ← ₹ 40

(C) ← ₹ 20   (D) ← ₹ 40

34. How much money is shown here?

(A) ₹ 23   (B) ₹ 23 and 50 p.

(C) ₹ 20 and 50 p.   (D) ₹ 21 and 50 p.

35. One toy car costs ₹ 10, How many toy cars can Dev buy for ₹ 35?

(A) 3   (B) 2   (C) 1   (D) 4

36. One ice-cream costs ₹ 20. How many ice-creams can Mona buy for ₹ 50?

(A) 3   (B) 4   (C) 2   (D) None of these

37. Which set of coin shows ₹ 3 ?

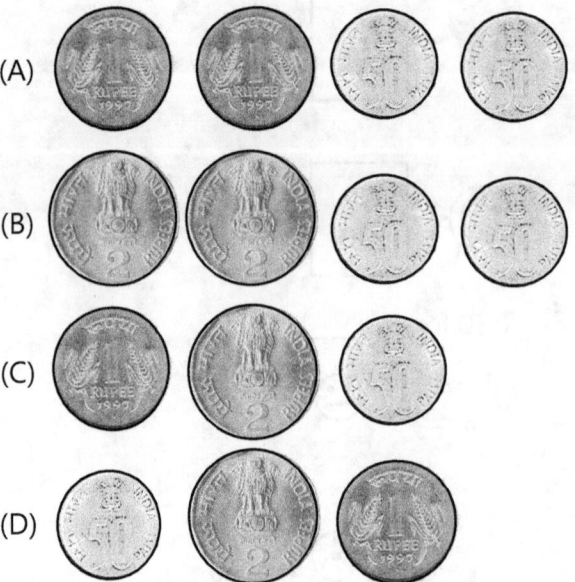

(A)

(B)

(C)

(D)

38. Which set shows ₹6?

(d) None of these

39.  ← ₹ 1   Balloon can be bought for

40. ₹ 3 = _____

(A) Four 50 Paise coins   (B)   Three 50 paise coins

(C) Six 50 paise coins   (D)   Two 25 paise coins

41. ✈ ← ₹ 5. This toy can be bought for

(A)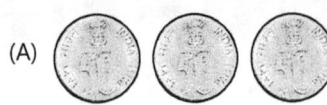

(B)

(C)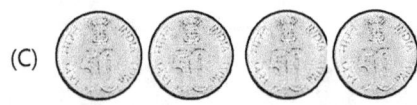

(D) None of these

42. ☎☎ ← ₹ 8   Soham gave ₹10 to buy this phone. How much will he get back?

(A) ₹ 10   (B) ₹ 18   (C) ₹ 2   (D) ₹ 5

43. ☺ ← ₹ 13. Rita gave ₹ 20 to buy this toy. How much will she get back?

(A) ₹ 33   (B) ₹ 3   (C) ₹ 23   (D) ₹ 7

44. Sam wants to exchange his ₹ 1 with some coins. Which set of coins he can take?

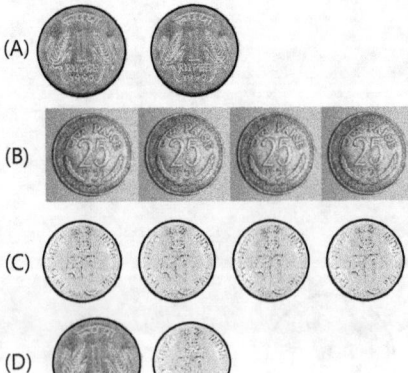

45. Sania wants to exchange her ₹ 2 with some coins. Which set of coins can she take?

(A) 50 P 50 P

(B) 25 P 25 P 25 P 25 P 25 P

(C) 50 P 50 P 50 P 50 P

(D) None of these

46. Which item has biggest, greatest or highest cost?

(A) ← ₹ 230   (B) ← ₹ 123

(C) ← ₹ 250   (D) ← ₹ 97

47. Which item has lowest, smallest or least cost?

(A) ← ₹ 146   (B) ← ₹ 264

(C) ← ₹ 210   (D) ← ₹ 120

48. Which amount is less than ₹ 90?

(A) ₹ 80 / ₹ 30   (B) ₹ 100

(C) ₹ 20 / ₹ 50   (D) ₹ 150

49. Which amount is less than ₹ 70?

(A) ₹ 48   (B) ₹ 50 / ₹ 40

(C) ₹ 30 / ₹ 50   (D) ₹ 90

50. ← ₹ 30 Sonu gave ₹ 50 to buy this. How much will she get back?

(A) ₹ 80   (B) ₹ 20   (C) ₹ 40   (D) ₹ 10

51. ☆ ← ₹ 11   Sham gave ₹ 20 to buy this. How much will he get back?

    (A) ₹ 20   (B) ₹ 31   (C) ₹ 40   (D) ₹ 9

52. Radha wants to buy  ← ₹ 15. She has ₹ 10. How much more is needed?

    (A) ₹ 20   (B) ₹ 15   (C) ₹ 5   (D) None of these

53. Rita wants to buy 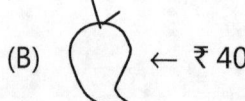 ₹ 75. She has ₹ 60. How much more is needed?

    (A) ₹ 30   (B) ₹ 25   (C) ₹ 15   (D) None of these

54. Roy pays ₹ 90 for the ✈ ← ₹ 50 and _____

    (A) 🍦 ← ₹ 10   (B) 🥭 ← ₹ 40

    (C) ☎ ← ₹ 60   (D) None of these

55. One book costs ₹ 30. How many books can Ram buy for ₹ 70?

    (A) 2   (B) 3   (C) 4   (D) 6

56. If one bag costs ₹ 20. How much does Tom need to pay for 3 bags?

    (A) ₹ 20   (B) ₹ 40   (C) ₹ 80   (D) ₹ 60

ANSWERSHEET

1.	Ⓐ Ⓑ Ⓒ Ⓓ	2.	Ⓐ Ⓑ Ⓒ Ⓓ	3.	Ⓐ Ⓑ Ⓒ Ⓓ	4.	Ⓐ Ⓑ Ⓒ Ⓓ
5.	Ⓐ Ⓑ Ⓒ Ⓓ	6.	Ⓐ Ⓑ Ⓒ Ⓓ	7.	Ⓐ Ⓑ Ⓒ Ⓓ	8.	Ⓐ Ⓑ Ⓒ Ⓓ
9.	Ⓐ Ⓑ Ⓒ Ⓓ	10.	Ⓐ Ⓑ Ⓒ Ⓓ	11.	Ⓐ Ⓑ Ⓒ Ⓓ	12.	Ⓐ Ⓑ Ⓒ Ⓓ
13.	Ⓐ Ⓑ Ⓒ Ⓓ	14.	Ⓐ Ⓑ Ⓒ Ⓓ	15.	Ⓐ Ⓑ Ⓒ Ⓓ	16.	Ⓐ Ⓑ Ⓒ Ⓓ
17.	Ⓐ Ⓑ Ⓒ Ⓓ	18.	Ⓐ Ⓑ Ⓒ Ⓓ	19.	Ⓐ Ⓑ Ⓒ Ⓓ	20.	Ⓐ Ⓑ Ⓒ Ⓓ
21.	Ⓐ Ⓑ Ⓒ Ⓓ	22.	Ⓐ Ⓑ Ⓒ Ⓓ	23.	Ⓐ Ⓑ Ⓒ Ⓓ	24.	Ⓐ Ⓑ Ⓒ Ⓓ
25.	Ⓐ Ⓑ Ⓒ Ⓓ	26.	Ⓐ Ⓑ Ⓒ Ⓓ	27.	Ⓐ Ⓑ Ⓒ Ⓓ	28.	Ⓐ Ⓑ Ⓒ Ⓓ
29.	Ⓐ Ⓑ Ⓒ Ⓓ	30.	Ⓐ Ⓑ Ⓒ Ⓓ	31.	Ⓐ Ⓑ Ⓒ Ⓓ	32.	Ⓐ Ⓑ Ⓒ Ⓓ
33.	Ⓐ Ⓑ Ⓒ Ⓓ	34.	Ⓐ Ⓑ Ⓒ Ⓓ	35.	Ⓐ Ⓑ Ⓒ Ⓓ	36.	Ⓐ Ⓑ Ⓒ Ⓓ
37.	Ⓐ Ⓑ Ⓒ Ⓓ	38.	Ⓐ Ⓑ Ⓒ Ⓓ	39.	Ⓐ Ⓑ Ⓒ Ⓓ	40.	Ⓐ Ⓑ Ⓒ Ⓓ
41.	Ⓐ Ⓑ Ⓒ Ⓓ	42.	Ⓐ Ⓑ Ⓒ Ⓓ	43.	Ⓐ Ⓑ Ⓒ Ⓓ	44.	Ⓐ Ⓑ Ⓒ Ⓓ
45.	Ⓐ Ⓑ Ⓒ Ⓓ	46.	Ⓐ Ⓑ Ⓒ Ⓓ	47.	Ⓐ Ⓑ Ⓒ Ⓓ	48.	Ⓐ Ⓑ Ⓒ Ⓓ
49.	Ⓐ Ⓑ Ⓒ Ⓓ	50.	Ⓐ Ⓑ Ⓒ Ⓓ	51.	Ⓐ Ⓑ Ⓒ Ⓓ	52.	Ⓐ Ⓑ Ⓒ Ⓓ
53.	Ⓐ Ⓑ Ⓒ Ⓓ	54.	Ⓐ Ⓑ Ⓒ Ⓓ	55.	Ⓐ Ⓑ Ⓒ Ⓓ	56.	Ⓐ Ⓑ Ⓒ Ⓓ
57.	Ⓐ Ⓑ Ⓒ Ⓓ	58.	Ⓐ Ⓑ Ⓒ Ⓓ	59.	Ⓐ Ⓑ Ⓒ Ⓓ	60.	Ⓐ Ⓑ Ⓒ Ⓓ
61.	Ⓐ Ⓑ Ⓒ Ⓓ	62.	Ⓐ Ⓑ Ⓒ Ⓓ	63.	Ⓐ Ⓑ Ⓒ Ⓓ	64.	Ⓐ Ⓑ Ⓒ Ⓓ
65.	Ⓐ Ⓑ Ⓒ Ⓓ	66.	Ⓐ Ⓑ Ⓒ Ⓓ	67.	Ⓐ Ⓑ Ⓒ Ⓓ	68.	Ⓐ Ⓑ Ⓒ Ⓓ
69.	Ⓐ Ⓑ Ⓒ Ⓓ	70.	Ⓐ Ⓑ Ⓒ Ⓓ	71.	Ⓐ Ⓑ Ⓒ Ⓓ	72.	Ⓐ Ⓑ Ⓒ Ⓓ
73.	Ⓐ Ⓑ Ⓒ Ⓓ	74.	Ⓐ Ⓑ Ⓒ Ⓓ	75.	Ⓐ Ⓑ Ⓒ Ⓓ	76.	Ⓐ Ⓑ Ⓒ Ⓓ
77.	Ⓐ Ⓑ Ⓒ Ⓓ	78.	Ⓐ Ⓑ Ⓒ Ⓓ	79.	Ⓐ Ⓑ Ⓒ Ⓓ	80.	Ⓐ Ⓑ Ⓒ Ⓓ
81.	Ⓐ Ⓑ Ⓒ Ⓓ	82.	Ⓐ Ⓑ Ⓒ Ⓓ	83.	Ⓐ Ⓑ Ⓒ Ⓓ	84.	Ⓐ Ⓑ Ⓒ Ⓓ
85.	Ⓐ Ⓑ Ⓒ Ⓓ	86.	Ⓐ Ⓑ Ⓒ Ⓓ	87.	Ⓐ Ⓑ Ⓒ Ⓓ	88.	Ⓐ Ⓑ Ⓒ Ⓓ
89.	Ⓐ Ⓑ Ⓒ Ⓓ	90.	Ⓐ Ⓑ Ⓒ Ⓓ	91.	Ⓐ Ⓑ Ⓒ Ⓓ	92.	Ⓐ Ⓑ Ⓒ Ⓓ
93.	Ⓐ Ⓑ Ⓒ Ⓓ	94.	Ⓐ Ⓑ Ⓒ Ⓓ	95.	Ⓐ Ⓑ Ⓒ Ⓓ	96.	Ⓐ Ⓑ Ⓒ Ⓓ
97.	Ⓐ Ⓑ Ⓒ Ⓓ	98.	Ⓐ Ⓑ Ⓒ Ⓓ	99.	Ⓐ Ⓑ Ⓒ Ⓓ	100.	Ⓐ Ⓑ Ⓒ Ⓓ

Chapter 5
GEOMETRY (Shapes and Patterns)

Choose the Correct Answer

Directions (1 to 4): See the picture and answer the questions.

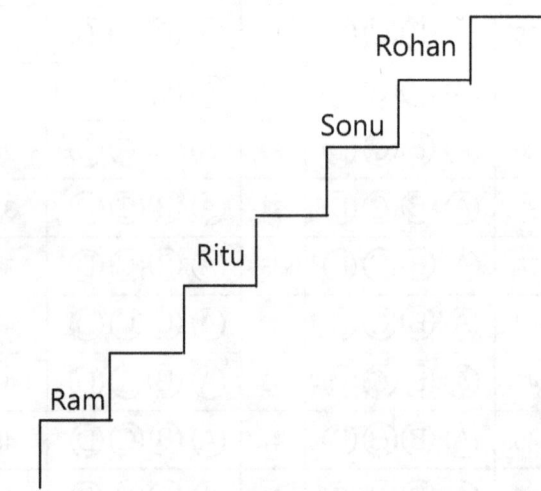

1.   Who is on top?

   (A) Ram   (B) Ritu   (C) Sonu   (D) Rohan

2.   Who is standing at the bottom?

   (A) Ram   (B) Ritu   (C) Sonu   (D) Rohan

3.   Who is standing above Sonu?

   (A) Ram   (B) Ritu   (C) Sonu   (D) Rohan

4.   Who is standing below Ritu?

   (A) Ram   (B) Ritu   (C) Sonu   (D) Rohan

5.   Which shape is a circle?

   (A)    (B) 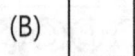   (C) 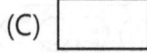   (D)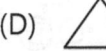

6. Which shape is a rectangle?

    (A)    (B)    (C)    (D) ▢

7. How many circles are there in the box?

    (A) 6   (B) 5

    (C) 2   (D) None

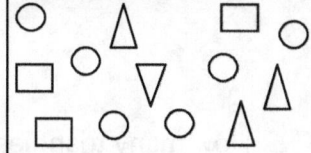

8)    Shape of the shaded part is

    (A) ▭   (B) △   (C) ⬭   (D) ▢

9) The figure is made up of how many triangles?

    (A) 8   (B) 9   (C) 10   (D) None of these

10. Which figure is not shown here?

    (A) Cube   (B) Cone   (C) Cylinder   (D) Sphere

11. A triangle has ____ sides .

    (A) Four   (B) Six   (C) Three   (D) None of these

12. Which shape is not shown here?

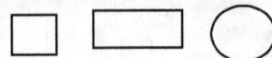

(A) Triangle   (B) Square   (C) Circle   (D) Rectangle

13) 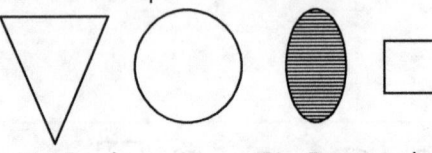   How many triangles are shown here?

(A) 3   (B) 4   (C) 6   (D) 5

14. Which shape is shaded below?

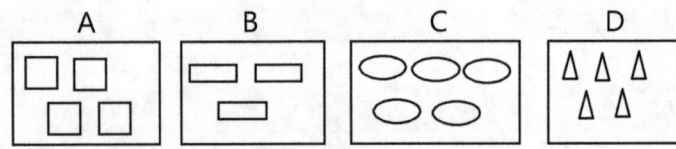

(A) Oval   (B) Rectangle   (C) Circle   (D) Triangle

15. Ram has 4 groups of shapes

In which group he will put oval?

(A) A   (B) B   (C) C   (D) D

16.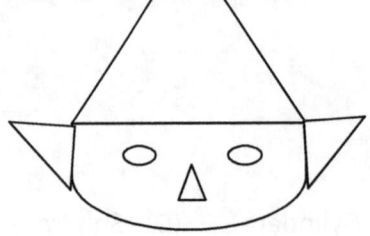

How many triangles are there in the adjoining figure?

(A) 5   (B) 4   (C) 6   (D) None of them

ANSWERSHEET

1. Ⓐ Ⓑ Ⓒ Ⓓ	2. Ⓐ Ⓑ Ⓒ Ⓓ	3. Ⓐ Ⓑ Ⓒ Ⓓ	4. Ⓐ Ⓑ Ⓒ Ⓓ
5. Ⓐ Ⓑ Ⓒ Ⓓ	6. Ⓐ Ⓑ Ⓒ Ⓓ	7. Ⓐ Ⓑ Ⓒ Ⓓ	8. Ⓐ Ⓑ Ⓒ Ⓓ
9. Ⓐ Ⓑ Ⓒ Ⓓ	10. Ⓐ Ⓑ Ⓒ Ⓓ	11. Ⓐ Ⓑ Ⓒ Ⓓ	12. Ⓐ Ⓑ Ⓒ Ⓓ
13. Ⓐ Ⓑ Ⓒ Ⓓ	14. Ⓐ Ⓑ Ⓒ Ⓓ	15. Ⓐ Ⓑ Ⓒ Ⓓ	16. Ⓐ Ⓑ Ⓒ Ⓓ
17. Ⓐ Ⓑ Ⓒ Ⓓ	18. Ⓐ Ⓑ Ⓒ Ⓓ	19. Ⓐ Ⓑ Ⓒ Ⓓ	20. Ⓐ Ⓑ Ⓒ Ⓓ
21. Ⓐ Ⓑ Ⓒ Ⓓ	22. Ⓐ Ⓑ Ⓒ Ⓓ	23. Ⓐ Ⓑ Ⓒ Ⓓ	24. Ⓐ Ⓑ Ⓒ Ⓓ
25. Ⓐ Ⓑ Ⓒ Ⓓ	26. Ⓐ Ⓑ Ⓒ Ⓓ	27. Ⓐ Ⓑ Ⓒ Ⓓ	28. Ⓐ Ⓑ Ⓒ Ⓓ
29. Ⓐ Ⓑ Ⓒ Ⓓ	30. Ⓐ Ⓑ Ⓒ Ⓓ	31. Ⓐ Ⓑ Ⓒ Ⓓ	32. Ⓐ Ⓑ Ⓒ Ⓓ
33. Ⓐ Ⓑ Ⓒ Ⓓ	34. Ⓐ Ⓑ Ⓒ Ⓓ	35. Ⓐ Ⓑ Ⓒ Ⓓ	36. Ⓐ Ⓑ Ⓒ Ⓓ
37. Ⓐ Ⓑ Ⓒ Ⓓ	38. Ⓐ Ⓑ Ⓒ Ⓓ	39. Ⓐ Ⓑ Ⓒ Ⓓ	40. Ⓐ Ⓑ Ⓒ Ⓓ
41. Ⓐ Ⓑ Ⓒ Ⓓ	42. Ⓐ Ⓑ Ⓒ Ⓓ	43. Ⓐ Ⓑ Ⓒ Ⓓ	44. Ⓐ Ⓑ Ⓒ Ⓓ
45. Ⓐ Ⓑ Ⓒ Ⓓ	46. Ⓐ Ⓑ Ⓒ Ⓓ	47. Ⓐ Ⓑ Ⓒ Ⓓ	48. Ⓐ Ⓑ Ⓒ Ⓓ
49. Ⓐ Ⓑ Ⓒ Ⓓ	50. Ⓐ Ⓑ Ⓒ Ⓓ	51. Ⓐ Ⓑ Ⓒ Ⓓ	52. Ⓐ Ⓑ Ⓒ Ⓓ
53. Ⓐ Ⓑ Ⓒ Ⓓ	54. Ⓐ Ⓑ Ⓒ Ⓓ	55. Ⓐ Ⓑ Ⓒ Ⓓ	56. Ⓐ Ⓑ Ⓒ Ⓓ
57. Ⓐ Ⓑ Ⓒ Ⓓ	58. Ⓐ Ⓑ Ⓒ Ⓓ	59. Ⓐ Ⓑ Ⓒ Ⓓ	60. Ⓐ Ⓑ Ⓒ Ⓓ
61. Ⓐ Ⓑ Ⓒ Ⓓ	62. Ⓐ Ⓑ Ⓒ Ⓓ	63. Ⓐ Ⓑ Ⓒ Ⓓ	64. Ⓐ Ⓑ Ⓒ Ⓓ
65. Ⓐ Ⓑ Ⓒ Ⓓ	66. Ⓐ Ⓑ Ⓒ Ⓓ	67. Ⓐ Ⓑ Ⓒ Ⓓ	68. Ⓐ Ⓑ Ⓒ Ⓓ
69. Ⓐ Ⓑ Ⓒ Ⓓ	70. Ⓐ Ⓑ Ⓒ Ⓓ	71. Ⓐ Ⓑ Ⓒ Ⓓ	72. Ⓐ Ⓑ Ⓒ Ⓓ
73. Ⓐ Ⓑ Ⓒ Ⓓ	74. Ⓐ Ⓑ Ⓒ Ⓓ	75. Ⓐ Ⓑ Ⓒ Ⓓ	76. Ⓐ Ⓑ Ⓒ Ⓓ
77. Ⓐ Ⓑ Ⓒ Ⓓ	78. Ⓐ Ⓑ Ⓒ Ⓓ	79. Ⓐ Ⓑ Ⓒ Ⓓ	80. Ⓐ Ⓑ Ⓒ Ⓓ
81. Ⓐ Ⓑ Ⓒ Ⓓ	82. Ⓐ Ⓑ Ⓒ Ⓓ	83. Ⓐ Ⓑ Ⓒ Ⓓ	84. Ⓐ Ⓑ Ⓒ Ⓓ
85. Ⓐ Ⓑ Ⓒ Ⓓ	86. Ⓐ Ⓑ Ⓒ Ⓓ	87. Ⓐ Ⓑ Ⓒ Ⓓ	88. Ⓐ Ⓑ Ⓒ Ⓓ
89. Ⓐ Ⓑ Ⓒ Ⓓ	90. Ⓐ Ⓑ Ⓒ Ⓓ	91. Ⓐ Ⓑ Ⓒ Ⓓ	92. Ⓐ Ⓑ Ⓒ Ⓓ
93. Ⓐ Ⓑ Ⓒ Ⓓ	94. Ⓐ Ⓑ Ⓒ Ⓓ	95. Ⓐ Ⓑ Ⓒ Ⓓ	96. Ⓐ Ⓑ Ⓒ Ⓓ
97. Ⓐ Ⓑ Ⓒ Ⓓ	98. Ⓐ Ⓑ Ⓒ Ⓓ	99. Ⓐ Ⓑ Ⓒ Ⓓ	100. Ⓐ Ⓑ Ⓒ Ⓓ

Chapter 6
LOGICAL AND ANALYTICAL REASONING

Choose the Correct Answer

1. Which is the next object?

    (A) ▭   (B) △   (C) ⬭   (D) None of these

2. Complete the pattern?

    (A) 35   (B) 30   (C) 20   (D) None of these

3. Which is the next object?

    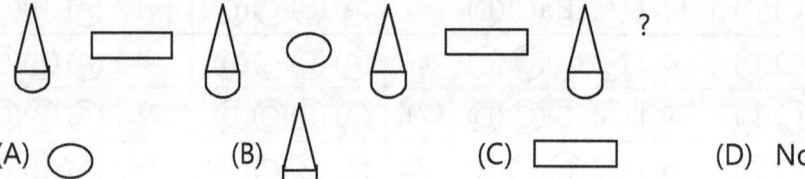

    (A) ◯   (B) ⬭   (C) ▭   (D) None of these

4. Which is the first ice-cream?

    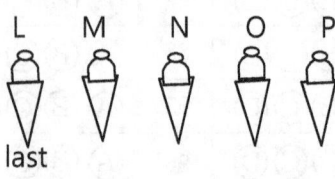

    last

    (A) M   (B) N   (C) O   (D) P

5.   Which is the next object?

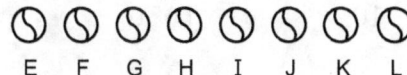 ?

(A) ▯   (B) ▢   (C) ▽   (D) ▽

6.   Ball 5th is before ball _____

1st ball

E   F   G   H   I   J   K   L

(A) H   (B) J   (C) G   (D) K

7.   [shape]   Which can be put together with this shape

to make a circle ?

(A) [shape]   (B) [shape]

(C) [shape]   (D) None of these

8.   If △ means '+' and '▽' means '_', Then 5 △ 5 = 15 ▽ __

(A) 10   (B) 5   (C) 15   (D) None of them

9.   If △ means '+' and '▽' means '−', then 2 △ 3 = 8 ▽ __

(A) 5   (B) 15   (C) 3   (D) None of them

10. If one '⊘' means '+' then 8 ⊘ 2 = 10 ⊘ ___

(A) 0   (B) 10   (C) 8   (D) 2

11. If one '▭' means '+' then 6 ▭ 2 = 8 ▭ __

    (A) 8   (B) 6   (C) 2   (D) 0

12. If one '△' means '+' then 10△ 4 = 8 △ __

    (A) 10   (B) 8   (C) 14   (D) 6

13. If one '◎' means '−' then 10 ◎ 4 = 6 ◎ __

    (A) 6   (B) 4   (C) 10   (D) 0

14. If one '▭' means '-' then 8 ▭ 2 = 9 ▭ __

    (A) 9   (B) 6   (C) 3   (D) None of them

15. If one '△' means '-' then 9 △ 4 = 10 △ __

    (A) 5   (B) 9   (C) 4   (D) 10

16. Which number will complete the pattern?

    | 2 | | 4 | | 6 | | 8 | | 10 | | ? |

    (A) 12   (B) 18   (C) 9   (D) None of them

17. Which is the next object?

    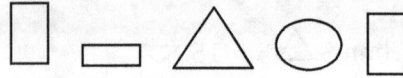

    (A) ▯   (B) △   (C) ◯   (D) ▭

18. Which is the next figure?

     ? ____

    (A) 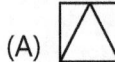   (B)    (C)   (D) ▭

19. Which is the next figure?

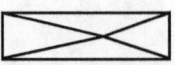    ?

(A) 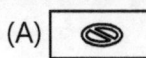   (B) 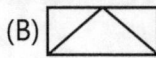   (C) 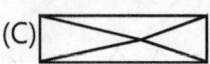   (D) [rectangle]

20) Complete the figures in questions 20 and 21.

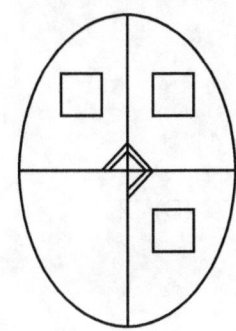

(A) 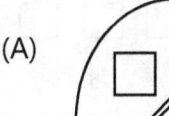   (B)

(C)    (D)

21.

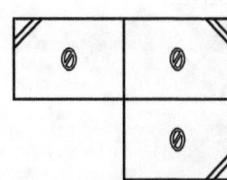

(A)    (B)

(C) [rectangle]   (D)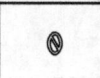

22. Which is the next object?

(A) [square]   (B) △   (C) [rectangle]   (D) ◯

23. △ 7th is after △ ___

1st Triangle

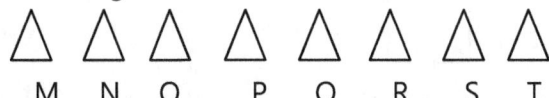

    M   N   O   P   Q   R   S   T

(A) R   (B) S   (C) T   (D) P

24)  Which can be put together with the shape to make a triangle?

(A) ⋁⋁⋁   (B) △△△   (C) ⋁⋁⋁   (D) None

25. How many squares will be there in pattern 4.

☐   ☐☐   ☐☐☐   ?

1   2   3   Pattern 4

(A) 5   (B) 4   (C) 3   (D) 2

26. How many △ will be there in pattern 5.

△   △△   △△△   △△△△   ?

1   2   3   4   Pattern 5

(A) △△△△   (B) △△△△△

(C) △△△   (D) △△

27. Which of the following options will continue the given series?

(A) ▭   (B) ▭   (C) ▯   (D) ▯

28. Complete the pattern

| 3 | 6 | 9 | 12 | ? |

(A) 13   (B) 15   (C) 16   (D) None of these

29. Complete the pattern

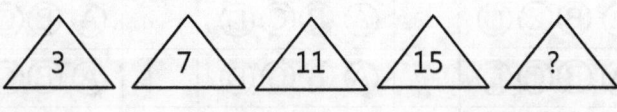

(A) 13   (B) 19   (C) 16   (D) None of these

30. Fill in the blanks

66, 68, ____ ,72, ____

(A) 74, 70   (B) 70, 74   (C) 69, 71   (D) None of these

ANSWERSHEET

1.	Ⓐ Ⓑ Ⓒ Ⓓ	2.	Ⓐ Ⓑ Ⓒ Ⓓ	3.	Ⓐ Ⓑ Ⓒ Ⓓ	4.	Ⓐ Ⓑ Ⓒ Ⓓ
5.	Ⓐ Ⓑ Ⓒ Ⓓ	6.	Ⓐ Ⓑ Ⓒ Ⓓ	7.	Ⓐ Ⓑ Ⓒ Ⓓ	8.	Ⓐ Ⓑ Ⓒ Ⓓ
9.	Ⓐ Ⓑ Ⓒ Ⓓ	10.	Ⓐ Ⓑ Ⓒ Ⓓ	11.	Ⓐ Ⓑ Ⓒ Ⓓ	12.	Ⓐ Ⓑ Ⓒ Ⓓ
13.	Ⓐ Ⓑ Ⓒ Ⓓ	14.	Ⓐ Ⓑ Ⓒ Ⓓ	15.	Ⓐ Ⓑ Ⓒ Ⓓ	16.	Ⓐ Ⓑ Ⓒ Ⓓ
17.	Ⓐ Ⓑ Ⓒ Ⓓ	18.	Ⓐ Ⓑ Ⓒ Ⓓ	19.	Ⓐ Ⓑ Ⓒ Ⓓ	20.	Ⓐ Ⓑ Ⓒ Ⓓ
21.	Ⓐ Ⓑ Ⓒ Ⓓ	22.	Ⓐ Ⓑ Ⓒ Ⓓ	23.	Ⓐ Ⓑ Ⓒ Ⓓ	24.	Ⓐ Ⓑ Ⓒ Ⓓ
25.	Ⓐ Ⓑ Ⓒ Ⓓ	26.	Ⓐ Ⓑ Ⓒ Ⓓ	27.	Ⓐ Ⓑ Ⓒ Ⓓ	28.	Ⓐ Ⓑ Ⓒ Ⓓ
29.	Ⓐ Ⓑ Ⓒ Ⓓ	30.	Ⓐ Ⓑ Ⓒ Ⓓ	31.	Ⓐ Ⓑ Ⓒ Ⓓ	32.	Ⓐ Ⓑ Ⓒ Ⓓ
33.	Ⓐ Ⓑ Ⓒ Ⓓ	34.	Ⓐ Ⓑ Ⓒ Ⓓ	35.	Ⓐ Ⓑ Ⓒ Ⓓ	36.	Ⓐ Ⓑ Ⓒ Ⓓ
37.	Ⓐ Ⓑ Ⓒ Ⓓ	38.	Ⓐ Ⓑ Ⓒ Ⓓ	39.	Ⓐ Ⓑ Ⓒ Ⓓ	40.	Ⓐ Ⓑ Ⓒ Ⓓ
41.	Ⓐ Ⓑ Ⓒ Ⓓ	42.	Ⓐ Ⓑ Ⓒ Ⓓ	43.	Ⓐ Ⓑ Ⓒ Ⓓ	44.	Ⓐ Ⓑ Ⓒ Ⓓ
45.	Ⓐ Ⓑ Ⓒ Ⓓ	46.	Ⓐ Ⓑ Ⓒ Ⓓ	47.	Ⓐ Ⓑ Ⓒ Ⓓ	48.	Ⓐ Ⓑ Ⓒ Ⓓ
49.	Ⓐ Ⓑ Ⓒ Ⓓ	50.	Ⓐ Ⓑ Ⓒ Ⓓ	51.	Ⓐ Ⓑ Ⓒ Ⓓ	52.	Ⓐ Ⓑ Ⓒ Ⓓ
53.	Ⓐ Ⓑ Ⓒ Ⓓ	54.	Ⓐ Ⓑ Ⓒ Ⓓ	55.	Ⓐ Ⓑ Ⓒ Ⓓ	56.	Ⓐ Ⓑ Ⓒ Ⓓ
57.	Ⓐ Ⓑ Ⓒ Ⓓ	58.	Ⓐ Ⓑ Ⓒ Ⓓ	59.	Ⓐ Ⓑ Ⓒ Ⓓ	60.	Ⓐ Ⓑ Ⓒ Ⓓ
61.	Ⓐ Ⓑ Ⓒ Ⓓ	62.	Ⓐ Ⓑ Ⓒ Ⓓ	63.	Ⓐ Ⓑ Ⓒ Ⓓ	64.	Ⓐ Ⓑ Ⓒ Ⓓ
65.	Ⓐ Ⓑ Ⓒ Ⓓ	66.	Ⓐ Ⓑ Ⓒ Ⓓ	67.	Ⓐ Ⓑ Ⓒ Ⓓ	68.	Ⓐ Ⓑ Ⓒ Ⓓ
69.	Ⓐ Ⓑ Ⓒ Ⓓ	70.	Ⓐ Ⓑ Ⓒ Ⓓ	71.	Ⓐ Ⓑ Ⓒ Ⓓ	72.	Ⓐ Ⓑ Ⓒ Ⓓ
73.	Ⓐ Ⓑ Ⓒ Ⓓ	74.	Ⓐ Ⓑ Ⓒ Ⓓ	75.	Ⓐ Ⓑ Ⓒ Ⓓ	76.	Ⓐ Ⓑ Ⓒ Ⓓ
77.	Ⓐ Ⓑ Ⓒ Ⓓ	78.	Ⓐ Ⓑ Ⓒ Ⓓ	79.	Ⓐ Ⓑ Ⓒ Ⓓ	80.	Ⓐ Ⓑ Ⓒ Ⓓ
81.	Ⓐ Ⓑ Ⓒ Ⓓ	82.	Ⓐ Ⓑ Ⓒ Ⓓ	83.	Ⓐ Ⓑ Ⓒ Ⓓ	84.	Ⓐ Ⓑ Ⓒ Ⓓ
85.	Ⓐ Ⓑ Ⓒ Ⓓ	86.	Ⓐ Ⓑ Ⓒ Ⓓ	87.	Ⓐ Ⓑ Ⓒ Ⓓ	88.	Ⓐ Ⓑ Ⓒ Ⓓ
89.	Ⓐ Ⓑ Ⓒ Ⓓ	90.	Ⓐ Ⓑ Ⓒ Ⓓ	91.	Ⓐ Ⓑ Ⓒ Ⓓ	92.	Ⓐ Ⓑ Ⓒ Ⓓ
93.	Ⓐ Ⓑ Ⓒ Ⓓ	94.	Ⓐ Ⓑ Ⓒ Ⓓ	95.	Ⓐ Ⓑ Ⓒ Ⓓ	96.	Ⓐ Ⓑ Ⓒ Ⓓ
97.	Ⓐ Ⓑ Ⓒ Ⓓ	98.	Ⓐ Ⓑ Ⓒ Ⓓ	99.	Ⓐ Ⓑ Ⓒ Ⓓ	100.	Ⓐ Ⓑ Ⓒ Ⓓ

Chapter 7
TIME

Topics: Hours and minutes hand, understanding correct time, time of the day. What part of the day is it, days of the week, months of the year.

Important Points

There are 12 months in a year.

There are 7 days in a week.

There are 24 hours in a day.

There are 60 minutes in a hour.

In a clock, the short hand is called the hour hand and the long hand is called the minute hand.

In 1 hour, the hour hand moves from one number to the next number on the clock.

Choose the Correct Answer

1.   What is the time in the clock?

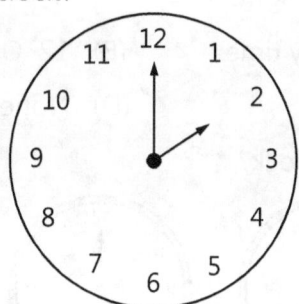

(A) 12 O' clock   (B) 2 O' clock   (C) 1 O' clock   (D) None of these

2.   What is the time in the clock?

(A) 8 O' clock   (B) 4 O' clock   (C) 11 O' clock   (C) None of these

3.　We go to school in the _____ .

(A) Night　　　　(B) Morning　　　　(C) Afternoon　　(D) Evening

4.　There are ___ days in a week.

(A) 9　　　　　　(B) 30　　　　　　(C) 7　　(D)　　12

5.　At 7 O' clock the hour hand will be at ____?

(A) 12　　　　　　(B) 7　　　　　　(C) both a and b　　(D) None of these

6.　Short hand is known as a _____.

(A) Hour hand　　(B) Minute hand　(C) My hand　　　(D) None of these

7.　_____ comes after Monday.

(A) Wednesday　(B) Sunday　　　　(C) Tuesday　　　(D) None of these

8.　There are ___ months in a year.

(A) 30　　　　　　(B) 7　　　　　　(C) 12　　　　　　(D) 365

9.　_____ is called mid-night.

(A) 12 O' clock in the day time　　(B) 12 O'clock at night

(C) 10 O'clock at night　　　　　　(D) None of these

10.　Which clock shows 8 O'clock?

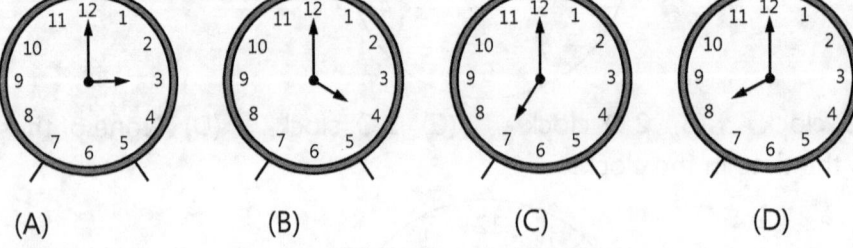

(A)　　　　　　(B)　　　　　　(C)　　　　　　(D)

11.　Which clock shows time less than 6 o' clock?

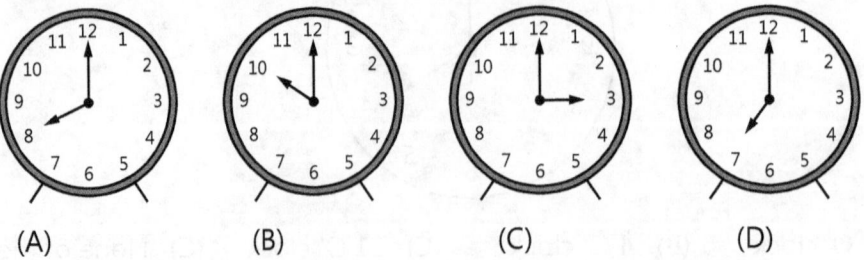

(A)　　　　　　(B)　　　　　　(C)　　　　　　(D)

12. We have dinner at _____

    (A) 8 O' clock in the morning   (B) 8 O' clock at night

    (C) 12 O' clock in day time   (D) None of these.

13. _____ comes after Saturday.

    (A) Sunday   (B) Monday   (C) Friday   (D) None of these

14. Month of November comes after _____.

    (A) December   (B) October   (C) September   (D) None of these

15. In a day there are _____ hours.

    (A) 30   (B) 24   (C) 365   (D) 12

16. In 1 hour, the hour hand moves from one number to the next number on the clock.

    (A) True   (B) False   (C) Can't say   (D) None of these

17. One hour before the time shown in the clock is _____

    (A) 11 O'clock   (B) 9 O'clock   (C) 8 O'clock   (D) None of these

18. Yesterday was Thursday, so today is _____.

    (A) Wednesday   (B) Tuesday   (C) Friday   (D) Saturday

19. Which is the 10th month of the year?

    (A) September   (B) October   (C) November   (D) December

20. Which date is the third Friday?

July						
S	M	T	W	T	F	S
					1	2
3	4	5	8	7	8	9
10	11	12	13	14	15	16
17	18	19	20	21	22	23
24	25	26	27	28	29	30
31						

    (A) 8 July   (B) 15 July   (C) 22 July   (D) 29 July

ANSWERSHEET

1. Ⓐ Ⓑ Ⓒ Ⓓ	2. Ⓐ Ⓑ Ⓒ Ⓓ	3. Ⓐ Ⓑ Ⓒ Ⓓ	4. Ⓐ Ⓑ Ⓒ Ⓓ
5. Ⓐ Ⓑ Ⓒ Ⓓ	6. Ⓐ Ⓑ Ⓒ Ⓓ	7. Ⓐ Ⓑ Ⓒ Ⓓ	8. Ⓐ Ⓑ Ⓒ Ⓓ
9. Ⓐ Ⓑ Ⓒ Ⓓ	10. Ⓐ Ⓑ Ⓒ Ⓓ	11. Ⓐ Ⓑ Ⓒ Ⓓ	12. Ⓐ Ⓑ Ⓒ Ⓓ
13. Ⓐ Ⓑ Ⓒ Ⓓ	14. Ⓐ Ⓑ Ⓒ Ⓓ	15. Ⓐ Ⓑ Ⓒ Ⓓ	16. Ⓐ Ⓑ Ⓒ Ⓓ
17. Ⓐ Ⓑ Ⓒ Ⓓ	18. Ⓐ Ⓑ Ⓒ Ⓓ	19. Ⓐ Ⓑ Ⓒ Ⓓ	20. Ⓐ Ⓑ Ⓒ Ⓓ
21. Ⓐ Ⓑ Ⓒ Ⓓ	22. Ⓐ Ⓑ Ⓒ Ⓓ	23. Ⓐ Ⓑ Ⓒ Ⓓ	24. Ⓐ Ⓑ Ⓒ Ⓓ
25. Ⓐ Ⓑ Ⓒ Ⓓ	26. Ⓐ Ⓑ Ⓒ Ⓓ	27. Ⓐ Ⓑ Ⓒ Ⓓ	28. Ⓐ Ⓑ Ⓒ Ⓓ
29. Ⓐ Ⓑ Ⓒ Ⓓ	30. Ⓐ Ⓑ Ⓒ Ⓓ	31. Ⓐ Ⓑ Ⓒ Ⓓ	32. Ⓐ Ⓑ Ⓒ Ⓓ
33. Ⓐ Ⓑ Ⓒ Ⓓ	34. Ⓐ Ⓑ Ⓒ Ⓓ	35. Ⓐ Ⓑ Ⓒ Ⓓ	36. Ⓐ Ⓑ Ⓒ Ⓓ
37. Ⓐ Ⓑ Ⓒ Ⓓ	38. Ⓐ Ⓑ Ⓒ Ⓓ	39. Ⓐ Ⓑ Ⓒ Ⓓ	40. Ⓐ Ⓑ Ⓒ Ⓓ
41. Ⓐ Ⓑ Ⓒ Ⓓ	42. Ⓐ Ⓑ Ⓒ Ⓓ	43. Ⓐ Ⓑ Ⓒ Ⓓ	44. Ⓐ Ⓑ Ⓒ Ⓓ
45. Ⓐ Ⓑ Ⓒ Ⓓ	46. Ⓐ Ⓑ Ⓒ Ⓓ	47. Ⓐ Ⓑ Ⓒ Ⓓ	48. Ⓐ Ⓑ Ⓒ Ⓓ
49. Ⓐ Ⓑ Ⓒ Ⓓ	50. Ⓐ Ⓑ Ⓒ Ⓓ	51. Ⓐ Ⓑ Ⓒ Ⓓ	52. Ⓐ Ⓑ Ⓒ Ⓓ
53. Ⓐ Ⓑ Ⓒ Ⓓ	54. Ⓐ Ⓑ Ⓒ Ⓓ	55. Ⓐ Ⓑ Ⓒ Ⓓ	56. Ⓐ Ⓑ Ⓒ Ⓓ
57. Ⓐ Ⓑ Ⓒ Ⓓ	58. Ⓐ Ⓑ Ⓒ Ⓓ	59. Ⓐ Ⓑ Ⓒ Ⓓ	60. Ⓐ Ⓑ Ⓒ Ⓓ
61. Ⓐ Ⓑ Ⓒ Ⓓ	62. Ⓐ Ⓑ Ⓒ Ⓓ	63. Ⓐ Ⓑ Ⓒ Ⓓ	64. Ⓐ Ⓑ Ⓒ Ⓓ
65. Ⓐ Ⓑ Ⓒ Ⓓ	66. Ⓐ Ⓑ Ⓒ Ⓓ	67. Ⓐ Ⓑ Ⓒ Ⓓ	68. Ⓐ Ⓑ Ⓒ Ⓓ
69. Ⓐ Ⓑ Ⓒ Ⓓ	70. Ⓐ Ⓑ Ⓒ Ⓓ	71. Ⓐ Ⓑ Ⓒ Ⓓ	72. Ⓐ Ⓑ Ⓒ Ⓓ
73. Ⓐ Ⓑ Ⓒ Ⓓ	74. Ⓐ Ⓑ Ⓒ Ⓓ	75. Ⓐ Ⓑ Ⓒ Ⓓ	76. Ⓐ Ⓑ Ⓒ Ⓓ
77. Ⓐ Ⓑ Ⓒ Ⓓ	78. Ⓐ Ⓑ Ⓒ Ⓓ	79. Ⓐ Ⓑ Ⓒ Ⓓ	80. Ⓐ Ⓑ Ⓒ Ⓓ
81. Ⓐ Ⓑ Ⓒ Ⓓ	82. Ⓐ Ⓑ Ⓒ Ⓓ	83. Ⓐ Ⓑ Ⓒ Ⓓ	84. Ⓐ Ⓑ Ⓒ Ⓓ
85. Ⓐ Ⓑ Ⓒ Ⓓ	86. Ⓐ Ⓑ Ⓒ Ⓓ	87. Ⓐ Ⓑ Ⓒ Ⓓ	88. Ⓐ Ⓑ Ⓒ Ⓓ
89. Ⓐ Ⓑ Ⓒ Ⓓ	90. Ⓐ Ⓑ Ⓒ Ⓓ	91. Ⓐ Ⓑ Ⓒ Ⓓ	92. Ⓐ Ⓑ Ⓒ Ⓓ
93. Ⓐ Ⓑ Ⓒ Ⓓ	94. Ⓐ Ⓑ Ⓒ Ⓓ	95. Ⓐ Ⓑ Ⓒ Ⓓ	96. Ⓐ Ⓑ Ⓒ Ⓓ
97. Ⓐ Ⓑ Ⓒ Ⓓ	98. Ⓐ Ⓑ Ⓒ Ⓓ	99. Ⓐ Ⓑ Ⓒ Ⓓ	100. Ⓐ Ⓑ Ⓒ Ⓓ

Chapter 8
MEASUREMENT

Choose the Correct Answer:

1.   Which is the longest hockey?

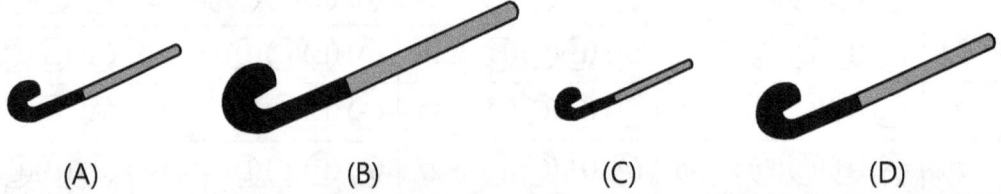

(A)   (B)   (C)   (D)

2.   Which bat is the tallest?

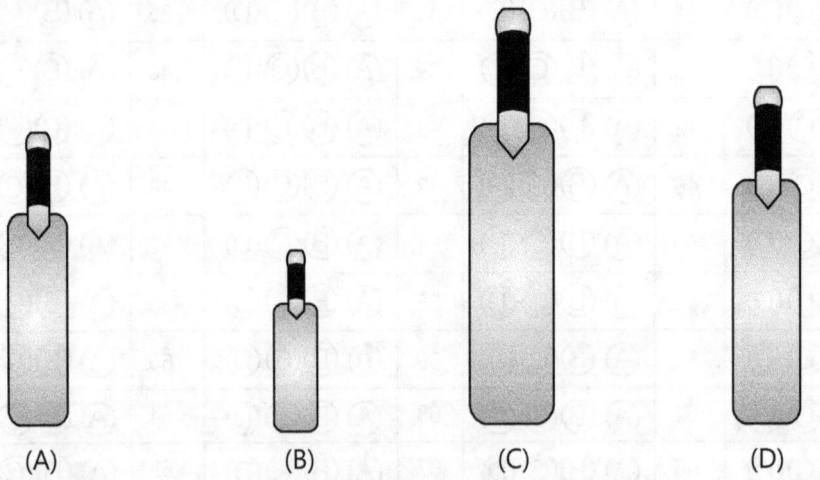

(A)   (B)   (C)   (D)

3.   Which is the thinnest glue stick?

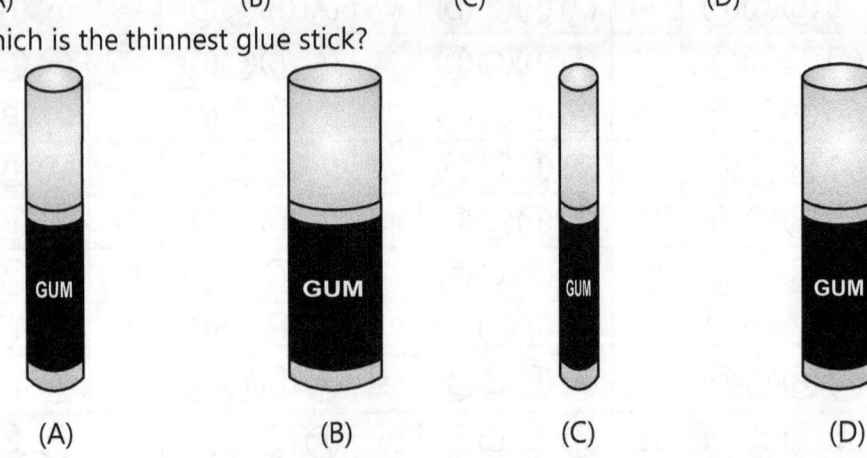

(A)   (B)   (C)   (D)

4. Which cat is closest to the milk?

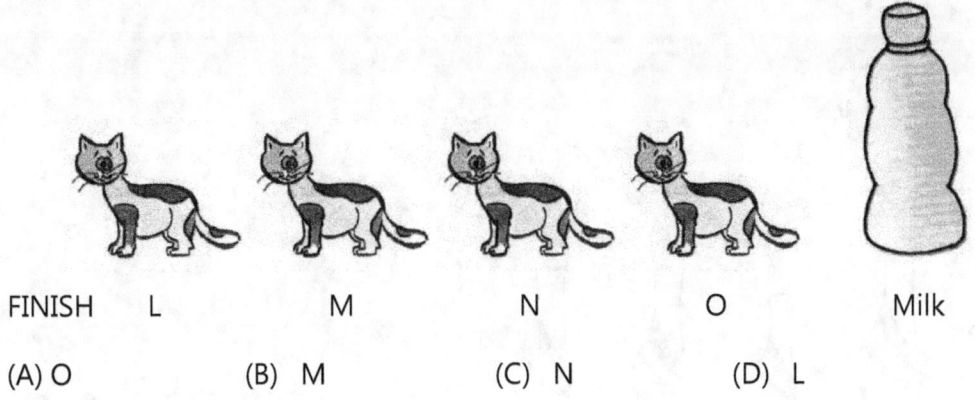

FINISH   L   M   N   O   Milk

(A) O   (B) M   (C) N   (D) L

5. Who is the heaviest?

P   Q   R   S

(A) P   (B) R   (C) Q   (D) Q and S

6. Which two cups are same in size?

L   M   N   O

(A) L and M   (B) N and O   (C) L and N   (D) M and O

7. Which vase is smaller than vase X?

    X

    (a)   (b)   (c)   (d)

8. Length is measured with a _____

    (A) Thermometer   (B) Ruler   (C) Weighing scale   (D) None of these

9. This is used to measure _____.

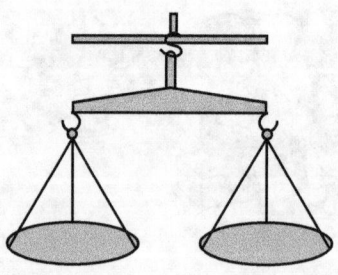

    (A) Length   (B) Height   (C) Weight   (D) None of these

10. Weight is measured with the help of _____

    (a) Thermometer   (B) Ruler

    (C) Weighing scale   (D) None of these

ANSWERSHEET

1.	Ⓐ Ⓑ Ⓒ Ⓓ	2.	Ⓐ Ⓑ Ⓒ Ⓓ	3.	Ⓐ Ⓑ Ⓒ Ⓓ	4.	Ⓐ Ⓑ Ⓒ Ⓓ
5.	Ⓐ Ⓑ Ⓒ Ⓓ	6.	Ⓐ Ⓑ Ⓒ Ⓓ	7.	Ⓐ Ⓑ Ⓒ Ⓓ	8.	Ⓐ Ⓑ Ⓒ Ⓓ
9.	Ⓐ Ⓑ Ⓒ Ⓓ	10.	Ⓐ Ⓑ Ⓒ Ⓓ	11.	Ⓐ Ⓑ Ⓒ Ⓓ	12.	Ⓐ Ⓑ Ⓒ Ⓓ
13.	Ⓐ Ⓑ Ⓒ Ⓓ	14.	Ⓐ Ⓑ Ⓒ Ⓓ	15.	Ⓐ Ⓑ Ⓒ Ⓓ	16.	Ⓐ Ⓑ Ⓒ Ⓓ
17.	Ⓐ Ⓑ Ⓒ Ⓓ	18.	Ⓐ Ⓑ Ⓒ Ⓓ	19.	Ⓐ Ⓑ Ⓒ Ⓓ	20.	Ⓐ Ⓑ Ⓒ Ⓓ
21.	Ⓐ Ⓑ Ⓒ Ⓓ	22.	Ⓐ Ⓑ Ⓒ Ⓓ	23.	Ⓐ Ⓑ Ⓒ Ⓓ	24.	Ⓐ Ⓑ Ⓒ Ⓓ
25.	Ⓐ Ⓑ Ⓒ Ⓓ	26.	Ⓐ Ⓑ Ⓒ Ⓓ	27.	Ⓐ Ⓑ Ⓒ Ⓓ	28.	Ⓐ Ⓑ Ⓒ Ⓓ
29.	Ⓐ Ⓑ Ⓒ Ⓓ	30.	Ⓐ Ⓑ Ⓒ Ⓓ	31.	Ⓐ Ⓑ Ⓒ Ⓓ	32.	Ⓐ Ⓑ Ⓒ Ⓓ
33.	Ⓐ Ⓑ Ⓒ Ⓓ	34.	Ⓐ Ⓑ Ⓒ Ⓓ	35.	Ⓐ Ⓑ Ⓒ Ⓓ	36.	Ⓐ Ⓑ Ⓒ Ⓓ
37.	Ⓐ Ⓑ Ⓒ Ⓓ	38.	Ⓐ Ⓑ Ⓒ Ⓓ	39.	Ⓐ Ⓑ Ⓒ Ⓓ	40.	Ⓐ Ⓑ Ⓒ Ⓓ
41.	Ⓐ Ⓑ Ⓒ Ⓓ	42.	Ⓐ Ⓑ Ⓒ Ⓓ	43.	Ⓐ Ⓑ Ⓒ Ⓓ	44.	Ⓐ Ⓑ Ⓒ Ⓓ
45.	Ⓐ Ⓑ Ⓒ Ⓓ	46.	Ⓐ Ⓑ Ⓒ Ⓓ	47.	Ⓐ Ⓑ Ⓒ Ⓓ	48.	Ⓐ Ⓑ Ⓒ Ⓓ
49.	Ⓐ Ⓑ Ⓒ Ⓓ	50.	Ⓐ Ⓑ Ⓒ Ⓓ	51.	Ⓐ Ⓑ Ⓒ Ⓓ	52.	Ⓐ Ⓑ Ⓒ Ⓓ
53.	Ⓐ Ⓑ Ⓒ Ⓓ	54.	Ⓐ Ⓑ Ⓒ Ⓓ	55.	Ⓐ Ⓑ Ⓒ Ⓓ	56.	Ⓐ Ⓑ Ⓒ Ⓓ
57.	Ⓐ Ⓑ Ⓒ Ⓓ	58.	Ⓐ Ⓑ Ⓒ Ⓓ	59.	Ⓐ Ⓑ Ⓒ Ⓓ	60.	Ⓐ Ⓑ Ⓒ Ⓓ
61.	Ⓐ Ⓑ Ⓒ Ⓓ	62.	Ⓐ Ⓑ Ⓒ Ⓓ	63.	Ⓐ Ⓑ Ⓒ Ⓓ	64.	Ⓐ Ⓑ Ⓒ Ⓓ
65.	Ⓐ Ⓑ Ⓒ Ⓓ	66.	Ⓐ Ⓑ Ⓒ Ⓓ	67.	Ⓐ Ⓑ Ⓒ Ⓓ	68.	Ⓐ Ⓑ Ⓒ Ⓓ
69.	Ⓐ Ⓑ Ⓒ Ⓓ	70.	Ⓐ Ⓑ Ⓒ Ⓓ	71.	Ⓐ Ⓑ Ⓒ Ⓓ	72.	Ⓐ Ⓑ Ⓒ Ⓓ
73.	Ⓐ Ⓑ Ⓒ Ⓓ	74.	Ⓐ Ⓑ Ⓒ Ⓓ	75.	Ⓐ Ⓑ Ⓒ Ⓓ	76.	Ⓐ Ⓑ Ⓒ Ⓓ
77.	Ⓐ Ⓑ Ⓒ Ⓓ	78.	Ⓐ Ⓑ Ⓒ Ⓓ	79.	Ⓐ Ⓑ Ⓒ Ⓓ	80.	Ⓐ Ⓑ Ⓒ Ⓓ
81.	Ⓐ Ⓑ Ⓒ Ⓓ	82.	Ⓐ Ⓑ Ⓒ Ⓓ	83.	Ⓐ Ⓑ Ⓒ Ⓓ	84.	Ⓐ Ⓑ Ⓒ Ⓓ
85.	Ⓐ Ⓑ Ⓒ Ⓓ	86.	Ⓐ Ⓑ Ⓒ Ⓓ	87.	Ⓐ Ⓑ Ⓒ Ⓓ	88.	Ⓐ Ⓑ Ⓒ Ⓓ
89.	Ⓐ Ⓑ Ⓒ Ⓓ	90.	Ⓐ Ⓑ Ⓒ Ⓓ	91.	Ⓐ Ⓑ Ⓒ Ⓓ	92.	Ⓐ Ⓑ Ⓒ Ⓓ
93.	Ⓐ Ⓑ Ⓒ Ⓓ	94.	Ⓐ Ⓑ Ⓒ Ⓓ	95.	Ⓐ Ⓑ Ⓒ Ⓓ	96.	Ⓐ Ⓑ Ⓒ Ⓓ
97.	Ⓐ Ⓑ Ⓒ Ⓓ	98.	Ⓐ Ⓑ Ⓒ Ⓓ	99.	Ⓐ Ⓑ Ⓒ Ⓓ	100.	Ⓐ Ⓑ Ⓒ Ⓓ

MODEL TEST PAPER 1

1. I have 8 sweets. Rishika gave me 3 more. Anushka gave me 4 more. How many sweets I have?

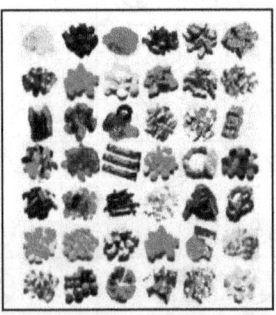

   (A) 8+2+3   (B) 4+3+7   (C) 8+3+4   (D) None of these

2. A shopkeeper sold 50 pens on Wednesday. He sold 8 pens less on Thursday. How many pens are sold on Thursday?

   (A) 50 – 8 = 40   (B) 50 – 42 = 8   (C) 50 – 8 = 42   (D) None of these

3. 7 tens 2 ones + 1 tens 9 ones =

   (A) 19   (B) 91   (C) 79   (D) None of these

4. $10 - \boxed{\vcenter{\hbox{⚅}}}$ =

   (A) 5   (B) 6   (C) 7   (D) None of these

5. Which is same as 15 – 9 =?

   (A) 10 – 6   (B) 12 – 6   (C) 20 – 2   (D) None of these

6. Which figure shows equal collection?

(A)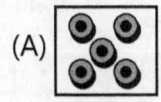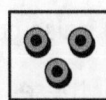

(B)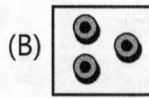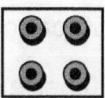

(C)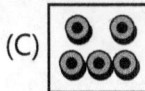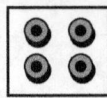

(D)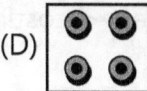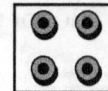

7. There are 8 ones and 9 tens in

(A) 98   (B) 89   (C) 80   (D) 90

8. 84 is same as

(A) 80 + 40   (B) 40+8   (C) 80+4   (D) None of these

9. Which box has more than 7 but less than 9 dots?

(A) 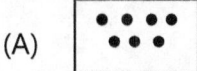 (B) 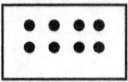 (C) 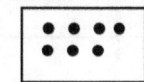 (D) None of these

10. Which numbers are arranged in ascending order?

(A) 20,32,14,10   (B) 81,18,88,80

(C) 09,19,90,99   (D) 42,44,24,22

11. Which number line shows counting by 2`s?

(A)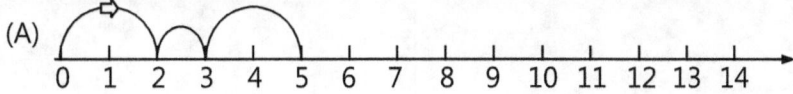

(B)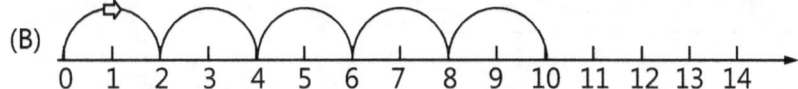

(C)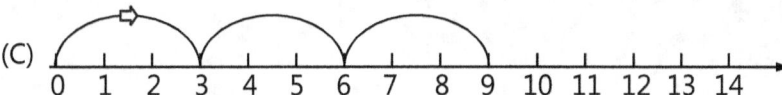

(D) None of these

12. ₹ 7 =

(A) ₹3 +₹ 4 (coins)   (B) ₹2 +₹ 5 (coins)

(C) ₹2 +₹ 6 (coins)   (D) None of these

13. ₹4 = ...

  (A) Eight 50 paise coins   (B) Five 50 paise coins

  (C) Four 50 paise coins   (D) None of these

14. Ram pays ₹80 for the  costing ₹ 30 and _____

  (A)  ₹ 20   (B)  ₹ 50

  (C)  ₹ 10   (D) None of these

15. Janhavi wants to exchange her ₹ 3 with some coins. Which set of coins she can take?

  (A)

  (B)

  (C)

  (D)

16. One toy car costs ₹30. How many toy cars Anushka can buy for ₹70?

(A) 1   (B) 6   (C) 2   (D) 3

17. Rujuta wants to buy a bag for ₹75. She has ₹ 40. How much more is needed?

(A) ₹30   (B) ₹45   (C) ₹35   (D) None of these

18. Which number will come next?

(3)   (6)   (9)   (12)   (?)

(A) 21   (B) 14   (C) 15   (D) None of these

19. Which is the first square?

| A | B | C | D | E |
Last

(A) A   (B) E   (C) B   (D) None of these

20. ₹ 4 = ...

(A) Five 50 paise coins   (B) Four 25 paise coins

(C) Four one rupee coins   (D) None of these

21 ₹ 3 = ... paise

(A) 30   (B) 300   (C) 03   (D) None of these

22. What shape is the ball?

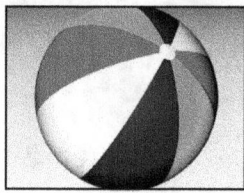

(A) Cylinder   (B) Cone

(C) Sphere   (D) Rectangle

23. Which box contains horizontal line?

(A) P   (B) Q   (C) R   (D) S

24. Which of the following shows descending or decreasing order?

(A) 98,89,99,91   (B) 42,24,12,02

(C) 84,89,97,98   (D) None of these

25. What is C's number?

A	B	C	D	E	F
49	34	86	91	27	44

(A) 30 + 4   (B) 80 + 5   (C) 80 + 6   (D) None of these

26. I am greater than 46 but less than 58. Who am I?

 <  <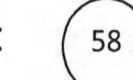

(A) 59   (B) 45   (C) 50   (D) None of these

27. Find the correct way to count by 2's.

    (A) 2,4,5,6,8   (B) 2,3,5,7,9

    (C) 1,2,4,6,8   (D) 0,2,4,6,8

28. Complete the number sentence

    8 + ☐ = 15

    (A) 6   (B) 9   (C) 4   (D) 7

29. Tanaya has 41 pencils. She gives 39 pencils to Janhavi. How many pencils are left?

    (A) 80   (B) 2   (C) 49   (D) None of these

30. Look at the alphabets given below. Which is the sixth from right ?

    Left   Right

        A   B   C   D   E   F   G   H   I   J   K   L   M   N   O   P   Q   R

    (A) F   (B) M   (C) J   (D) R

31. Which figure would come next in the pattern below?

    ◯ △ △ ◯ ☐ ☐ ◯ ☐ ☐ ◯ ✦✦ ◯ ☐

    (A) ☐   (B) ◯   (C) △   (D) None of these

32. Which is the 9th month of the year?

    (A) July   (B) August

    (C) September   (D) None of these

33. Which of the following would you use to hold milk?

    (A) Cup   (B) Table   (C) Pen Stand   (D) Net

34. How many bundles of 10 pencils can be made from 60 pencils?

(A) 8   (B) 6   (C) 5   (D) None of these

35. Veda has 28 figs and Hrishika has 39 Figs. How many figs do they have in all?

(A) 67   (B) 40   (C) 97   (D) None of these

ANSWERSHEET

1. Ⓐ Ⓑ Ⓒ Ⓓ	2. Ⓐ Ⓑ Ⓒ Ⓓ	3. Ⓐ Ⓑ Ⓒ Ⓓ	4. Ⓐ Ⓑ Ⓒ Ⓓ
5. Ⓐ Ⓑ Ⓒ Ⓓ	6. Ⓐ Ⓑ Ⓒ Ⓓ	7. Ⓐ Ⓑ Ⓒ Ⓓ	8. Ⓐ Ⓑ Ⓒ Ⓓ
9. Ⓐ Ⓑ Ⓒ Ⓓ	10. Ⓐ Ⓑ Ⓒ Ⓓ	11. Ⓐ Ⓑ Ⓒ Ⓓ	12. Ⓐ Ⓑ Ⓒ Ⓓ
13. Ⓐ Ⓑ Ⓒ Ⓓ	14. Ⓐ Ⓑ Ⓒ Ⓓ	15. Ⓐ Ⓑ Ⓒ Ⓓ	16. Ⓐ Ⓑ Ⓒ Ⓓ
17. Ⓐ Ⓑ Ⓒ Ⓓ	18. Ⓐ Ⓑ Ⓒ Ⓓ	19. Ⓐ Ⓑ Ⓒ Ⓓ	20. Ⓐ Ⓑ Ⓒ Ⓓ
21. Ⓐ Ⓑ Ⓒ Ⓓ	22. Ⓐ Ⓑ Ⓒ Ⓓ	23. Ⓐ Ⓑ Ⓒ Ⓓ	24. Ⓐ Ⓑ Ⓒ Ⓓ
25. Ⓐ Ⓑ Ⓒ Ⓓ	26. Ⓐ Ⓑ Ⓒ Ⓓ	27. Ⓐ Ⓑ Ⓒ Ⓓ	28. Ⓐ Ⓑ Ⓒ Ⓓ
29. Ⓐ Ⓑ Ⓒ Ⓓ	30. Ⓐ Ⓑ Ⓒ Ⓓ	31. Ⓐ Ⓑ Ⓒ Ⓓ	32. Ⓐ Ⓑ Ⓒ Ⓓ
33. Ⓐ Ⓑ Ⓒ Ⓓ	34. Ⓐ Ⓑ Ⓒ Ⓓ	35. Ⓐ Ⓑ Ⓒ Ⓓ	36. Ⓐ Ⓑ Ⓒ Ⓓ
37. Ⓐ Ⓑ Ⓒ Ⓓ	38. Ⓐ Ⓑ Ⓒ Ⓓ	39. Ⓐ Ⓑ Ⓒ Ⓓ	40. Ⓐ Ⓑ Ⓒ Ⓓ
41. Ⓐ Ⓑ Ⓒ Ⓓ	42. Ⓐ Ⓑ Ⓒ Ⓓ	43. Ⓐ Ⓑ Ⓒ Ⓓ	44. Ⓐ Ⓑ Ⓒ Ⓓ
45. Ⓐ Ⓑ Ⓒ Ⓓ	46. Ⓐ Ⓑ Ⓒ Ⓓ	47. Ⓐ Ⓑ Ⓒ Ⓓ	48. Ⓐ Ⓑ Ⓒ Ⓓ
49. Ⓐ Ⓑ Ⓒ Ⓓ	50. Ⓐ Ⓑ Ⓒ Ⓓ	51. Ⓐ Ⓑ Ⓒ Ⓓ	52. Ⓐ Ⓑ Ⓒ Ⓓ
53. Ⓐ Ⓑ Ⓒ Ⓓ	54. Ⓐ Ⓑ Ⓒ Ⓓ	55. Ⓐ Ⓑ Ⓒ Ⓓ	56. Ⓐ Ⓑ Ⓒ Ⓓ
57. Ⓐ Ⓑ Ⓒ Ⓓ	58. Ⓐ Ⓑ Ⓒ Ⓓ	59. Ⓐ Ⓑ Ⓒ Ⓓ	60. Ⓐ Ⓑ Ⓒ Ⓓ
61. Ⓐ Ⓑ Ⓒ Ⓓ	62. Ⓐ Ⓑ Ⓒ Ⓓ	63. Ⓐ Ⓑ Ⓒ Ⓓ	64. Ⓐ Ⓑ Ⓒ Ⓓ
65. Ⓐ Ⓑ Ⓒ Ⓓ	66. Ⓐ Ⓑ Ⓒ Ⓓ	67. Ⓐ Ⓑ Ⓒ Ⓓ	68. Ⓐ Ⓑ Ⓒ Ⓓ
69. Ⓐ Ⓑ Ⓒ Ⓓ	70. Ⓐ Ⓑ Ⓒ Ⓓ	71. Ⓐ Ⓑ Ⓒ Ⓓ	72. Ⓐ Ⓑ Ⓒ Ⓓ
73. Ⓐ Ⓑ Ⓒ Ⓓ	74. Ⓐ Ⓑ Ⓒ Ⓓ	75. Ⓐ Ⓑ Ⓒ Ⓓ	76. Ⓐ Ⓑ Ⓒ Ⓓ
77. Ⓐ Ⓑ Ⓒ Ⓓ	78. Ⓐ Ⓑ Ⓒ Ⓓ	79. Ⓐ Ⓑ Ⓒ Ⓓ	80. Ⓐ Ⓑ Ⓒ Ⓓ
81. Ⓐ Ⓑ Ⓒ Ⓓ	82. Ⓐ Ⓑ Ⓒ Ⓓ	83. Ⓐ Ⓑ Ⓒ Ⓓ	84. Ⓐ Ⓑ Ⓒ Ⓓ
85. Ⓐ Ⓑ Ⓒ Ⓓ	86. Ⓐ Ⓑ Ⓒ Ⓓ	87. Ⓐ Ⓑ Ⓒ Ⓓ	88. Ⓐ Ⓑ Ⓒ Ⓓ
89. Ⓐ Ⓑ Ⓒ Ⓓ	90. Ⓐ Ⓑ Ⓒ Ⓓ	91. Ⓐ Ⓑ Ⓒ Ⓓ	92. Ⓐ Ⓑ Ⓒ Ⓓ
93. Ⓐ Ⓑ Ⓒ Ⓓ	94. Ⓐ Ⓑ Ⓒ Ⓓ	95. Ⓐ Ⓑ Ⓒ Ⓓ	96. Ⓐ Ⓑ Ⓒ Ⓓ
97. Ⓐ Ⓑ Ⓒ Ⓓ	98. Ⓐ Ⓑ Ⓒ Ⓓ	99. Ⓐ Ⓑ Ⓒ Ⓓ	100. Ⓐ Ⓑ Ⓒ Ⓓ

MODEL TEST PAPER 2

1. Anushka had 33 books. Rujuta gave her 49 more. How many books does she have now?

    (A) 16   (B) 82   (C) 80   (D) None of these

2. Bhoomi and Sai picked 21 apples together. If Sai picked 14 apples, how many did Bhoomi pick?

    (A) 8   (B) 35   (C) 7   (D) None of these

3. | 97 | 43 | 84 | 98 | 67 |

        L   M   N   O   P

    What is P's number?

    (A) 80 + 4   (B) 60 + 7   (C) 40 + 3   (D) 90 + 7

4. The furniture store sold 9 tables, 13 book shelves and 18 beds. How many pieces of furniture did the store sell in all?

    (A) 31   (B) 21   (C) 40   (D) None of these

5. Cost of a toy is ₹34. Janhavi gave ₹ 50 note to the shopkeeper. How much money will she get back?

(A) ₹6   (B) ₹16   (C) ₹61   (D) None of these

6.

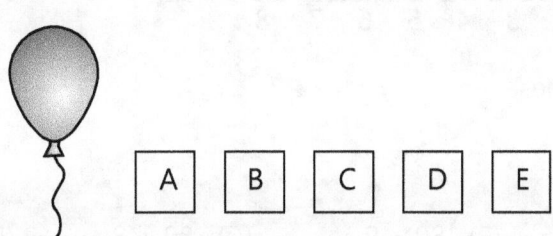

Which box is farthest from the balloon?

(A) A   (B) D   (C) E   (D) None of these

7. How many bundles of 10 pens can be made from 50 pens?

(A) 4   (B) 5   (C) 10   (D) None of these

8. Which of the following shows increasing or ascending order?

(A) 09, 90, 91, 99   (B) 44, 41, 84, 94

(C) 87, 21, 93, 100   (D) None of these

9. Which abacus shows 3 more than 49?

(A) 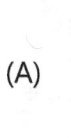   (B)    (C)   (D) None of these

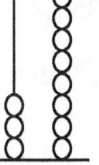
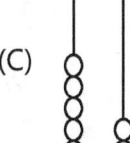

10. Which one is more than 97 but less than 99?

    (A) 90   (B) 98   (C) 100   (D) None of these

11. Which number line shows counting by 3's?

    (A)
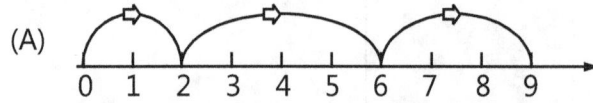

    (B)
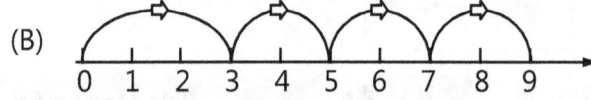

    (C)
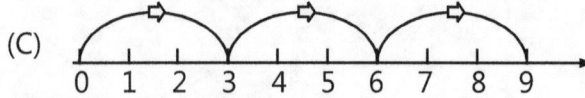

    (D) None of these

12. 89 is same as

    (A) 90 + 8   (B) 80 + 9   (C) 80 + 8   (D) None of these

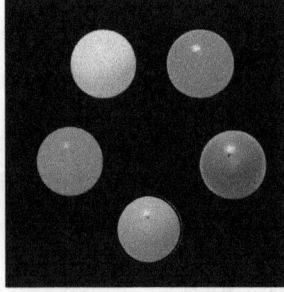

13.

    Which statement is true?

    (A) Balls are less than squares   (B) Balls are equal to squares

    (C) Squares are less than balls   (D) Squares are more than balls.

14. There are 4 ones and 3 tens in

    (A) 34   (B) 43   (C) 30   (D) None of these

15. There are 9 ones and 0 tens is the same as

(A) 90   (B) 99   (C) 9   (D) None of these

16. 8 ones and 4 tens is the same as

(A) 84   (B) 44   (C) 48   (C) 88

17. 3 more than 6 is represented by which number line?

(A)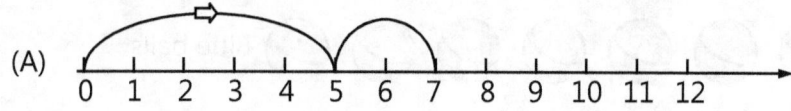

(B)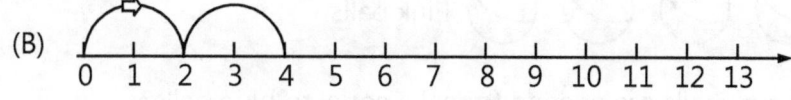

(C)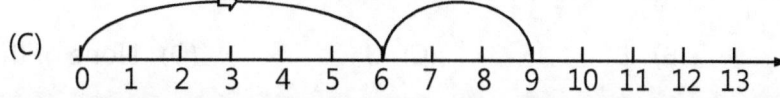

(D) None of these

18. 3 tens + 4 tens = ...

(A) 70 tens   (B) 77 tens   (C) 7 tens   (D) None of these

19. 3 more than 46 + 19

(A) 22   (B) 68   (C) 65   (D) None of these

20. 2 tens + 6 tens = ...

(A) 6 tens   (B) 66   (C) 60 tens   (D) None of these

21. How many balls should be crossed 'X' to show 8 − 3 = 5?

(A) 8   (B) 3   (C) 5   (D) None of these

22. Take away 2 from 6 to give

    (A) 16   (B) 8   (C) 4   (D) None of these

23. $10 -$ 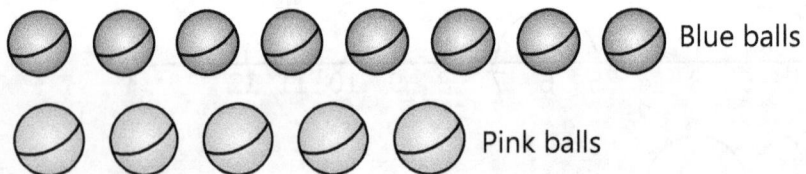 $= \ldots\ldots$

    (A) 6   (B) 16   (C) 4   (D) None of these

24.

Blue balls

Pink balls

How many pink balls are needed to make equal to blue balls?

    (A) 4   (B) 8   (C) 3   (D) None of these

25. Which of the following is another way of 5 less than 9?

    (A) $9 - 4 = 5$ (B) $14 - 9 = 5$ (C) $9 - 5 = 4$ (D) None of these

26. Which is same as $19 - 4$?

    (A) $12 - 4$ (B) $20 - 5$ (C) $21 - 7$ (D) None of these

27. There are 21 bugs, 15 bugs went away. How many bugs are left?

    (A) 6   (B) 16   (C) 36   (D) None of these

28. Dice's side is a _____.

    (A) Square   (B) Cone   (C) Cuboids   (D) Cube

29. Which figure is not shown here?

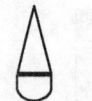

(A) Cone   (B) Cylinder   (C) Sphere   (D) Cube

30. Which of the following looks like a cone?

(A) A ball   (B) A dice

(C) An ice – cream cone   (D) Pencil box

31. If '△' means '+' and '▽' means '–' then 6 △ 4 = 20 ▽ ___

(A) 10   (B) 20   (C) 15   (D) None of these

32. If '△' means '+' and '▽' means '–' then 5 △ 3 = 11 ▽ ___

(A) 8   (B) 3   (C) 15   (D) None of these

33. Tanaya pays ₹50 for the ball of ₹ 20 and _____.

(A)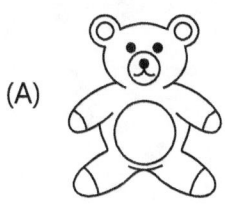
Teddy ₹ 40

(B)
Bell ₹ 30

(C)
Compass box ₹ 15

(D)
Bell ₹ 30

34. Janhavi pays ₹80 for the ₹50 pen and _____.

(A) 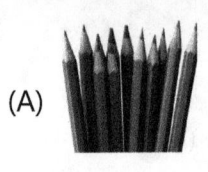 Pencil ₹ 20

(B) 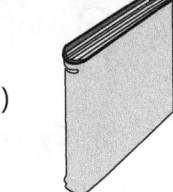 Book ₹ 30

(C) 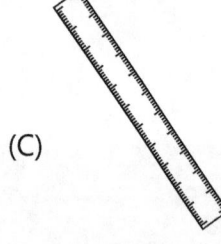 Scale ₹ 10

(D) 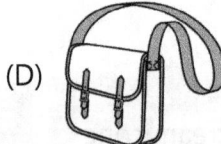 Bag ₹ 50

35. Anushka pays ₹70 for the bag of ₹ 30 and _____

(A) Marker Pen ₹ 50   (B) Pencil box ₹ 40

(C) Ball pens ₹ 20   (D) Book ₹ 10

ANSWERSHEET

1.	Ⓐ Ⓑ Ⓒ Ⓓ	2.	Ⓐ Ⓑ Ⓒ Ⓓ	3.	Ⓐ Ⓑ Ⓒ Ⓓ	4.	Ⓐ Ⓑ Ⓒ Ⓓ
5.	Ⓐ Ⓑ Ⓒ Ⓓ	6.	Ⓐ Ⓑ Ⓒ Ⓓ	7.	Ⓐ Ⓑ Ⓒ Ⓓ	8.	Ⓐ Ⓑ Ⓒ Ⓓ
9.	Ⓐ Ⓑ Ⓒ Ⓓ	10.	Ⓐ Ⓑ Ⓒ Ⓓ	11.	Ⓐ Ⓑ Ⓒ Ⓓ	12.	Ⓐ Ⓑ Ⓒ Ⓓ
13.	Ⓐ Ⓑ Ⓒ Ⓓ	14.	Ⓐ Ⓑ Ⓒ Ⓓ	15.	Ⓐ Ⓑ Ⓒ Ⓓ	16.	Ⓐ Ⓑ Ⓒ Ⓓ
17.	Ⓐ Ⓑ Ⓒ Ⓓ	18.	Ⓐ Ⓑ Ⓒ Ⓓ	19.	Ⓐ Ⓑ Ⓒ Ⓓ	20.	Ⓐ Ⓑ Ⓒ Ⓓ
21.	Ⓐ Ⓑ Ⓒ Ⓓ	22.	Ⓐ Ⓑ Ⓒ Ⓓ	23.	Ⓐ Ⓑ Ⓒ Ⓓ	24.	Ⓐ Ⓑ Ⓒ Ⓓ
25.	Ⓐ Ⓑ Ⓒ Ⓓ	26.	Ⓐ Ⓑ Ⓒ Ⓓ	27.	Ⓐ Ⓑ Ⓒ Ⓓ	28.	Ⓐ Ⓑ Ⓒ Ⓓ
29.	Ⓐ Ⓑ Ⓒ Ⓓ	30.	Ⓐ Ⓑ Ⓒ Ⓓ	31.	Ⓐ Ⓑ Ⓒ Ⓓ	32.	Ⓐ Ⓑ Ⓒ Ⓓ
33.	Ⓐ Ⓑ Ⓒ Ⓓ	34.	Ⓐ Ⓑ Ⓒ Ⓓ	35.	Ⓐ Ⓑ Ⓒ Ⓓ	36.	Ⓐ Ⓑ Ⓒ Ⓓ
37.	Ⓐ Ⓑ Ⓒ Ⓓ	38.	Ⓐ Ⓑ Ⓒ Ⓓ	39.	Ⓐ Ⓑ Ⓒ Ⓓ	40.	Ⓐ Ⓑ Ⓒ Ⓓ
41.	Ⓐ Ⓑ Ⓒ Ⓓ	42.	Ⓐ Ⓑ Ⓒ Ⓓ	43.	Ⓐ Ⓑ Ⓒ Ⓓ	44.	Ⓐ Ⓑ Ⓒ Ⓓ
45.	Ⓐ Ⓑ Ⓒ Ⓓ	46.	Ⓐ Ⓑ Ⓒ Ⓓ	47.	Ⓐ Ⓑ Ⓒ Ⓓ	48.	Ⓐ Ⓑ Ⓒ Ⓓ
49.	Ⓐ Ⓑ Ⓒ Ⓓ	50.	Ⓐ Ⓑ Ⓒ Ⓓ	51.	Ⓐ Ⓑ Ⓒ Ⓓ	52.	Ⓐ Ⓑ Ⓒ Ⓓ
53.	Ⓐ Ⓑ Ⓒ Ⓓ	54.	Ⓐ Ⓑ Ⓒ Ⓓ	55.	Ⓐ Ⓑ Ⓒ Ⓓ	56.	Ⓐ Ⓑ Ⓒ Ⓓ
57.	Ⓐ Ⓑ Ⓒ Ⓓ	58.	Ⓐ Ⓑ Ⓒ Ⓓ	59.	Ⓐ Ⓑ Ⓒ Ⓓ	60.	Ⓐ Ⓑ Ⓒ Ⓓ
61.	Ⓐ Ⓑ Ⓒ Ⓓ	62.	Ⓐ Ⓑ Ⓒ Ⓓ	63.	Ⓐ Ⓑ Ⓒ Ⓓ	64.	Ⓐ Ⓑ Ⓒ Ⓓ
65.	Ⓐ Ⓑ Ⓒ Ⓓ	66.	Ⓐ Ⓑ Ⓒ Ⓓ	67.	Ⓐ Ⓑ Ⓒ Ⓓ	68.	Ⓐ Ⓑ Ⓒ Ⓓ
69.	Ⓐ Ⓑ Ⓒ Ⓓ	70.	Ⓐ Ⓑ Ⓒ Ⓓ	71.	Ⓐ Ⓑ Ⓒ Ⓓ	72.	Ⓐ Ⓑ Ⓒ Ⓓ
73.	Ⓐ Ⓑ Ⓒ Ⓓ	74.	Ⓐ Ⓑ Ⓒ Ⓓ	75.	Ⓐ Ⓑ Ⓒ Ⓓ	76.	Ⓐ Ⓑ Ⓒ Ⓓ
77.	Ⓐ Ⓑ Ⓒ Ⓓ	78.	Ⓐ Ⓑ Ⓒ Ⓓ	79.	Ⓐ Ⓑ Ⓒ Ⓓ	80.	Ⓐ Ⓑ Ⓒ Ⓓ
81.	Ⓐ Ⓑ Ⓒ Ⓓ	82.	Ⓐ Ⓑ Ⓒ Ⓓ	83.	Ⓐ Ⓑ Ⓒ Ⓓ	84.	Ⓐ Ⓑ Ⓒ Ⓓ
85.	Ⓐ Ⓑ Ⓒ Ⓓ	86.	Ⓐ Ⓑ Ⓒ Ⓓ	87.	Ⓐ Ⓑ Ⓒ Ⓓ	88.	Ⓐ Ⓑ Ⓒ Ⓓ
89.	Ⓐ Ⓑ Ⓒ Ⓓ	90.	Ⓐ Ⓑ Ⓒ Ⓓ	91.	Ⓐ Ⓑ Ⓒ Ⓓ	92.	Ⓐ Ⓑ Ⓒ Ⓓ
93.	Ⓐ Ⓑ Ⓒ Ⓓ	94.	Ⓐ Ⓑ Ⓒ Ⓓ	95.	Ⓐ Ⓑ Ⓒ Ⓓ	96.	Ⓐ Ⓑ Ⓒ Ⓓ
97.	Ⓐ Ⓑ Ⓒ Ⓓ	98.	Ⓐ Ⓑ Ⓒ Ⓓ	99.	Ⓐ Ⓑ Ⓒ Ⓓ	100.	Ⓐ Ⓑ Ⓒ Ⓓ

MODEL TEST PAPER 3

1. If one ' ☐ ' means + then

    7 ☐ 5 =   10 ☐ __

    (A) 12   (B) 2   (C) 15   (D) None of these

2. Which is the next figure?

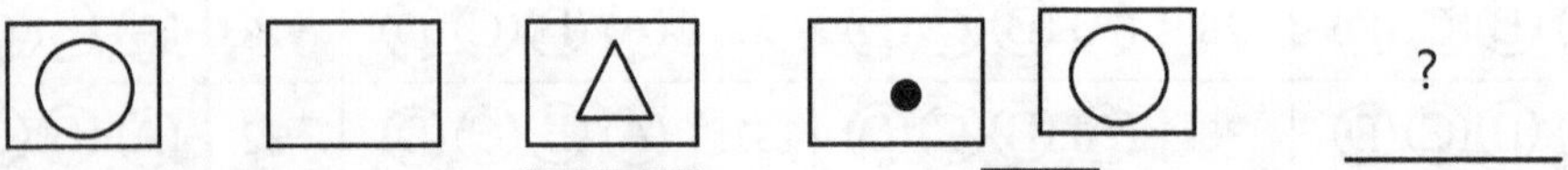

    (A) 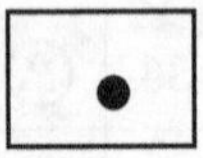   (B)    (C) 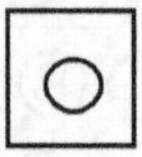   (D)

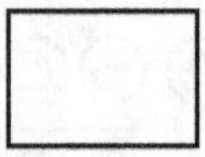

3. Complete the pattern

    (A) 20   (B) 21   (C) 22   (D) 25

4. Which number completes both the number sentences?

    45 + ☐ = 60 and 80 – ☐ = 65

    (A) 15   (B) 30   (C) 40   (D) None of these

5. Which number completes both the number sentences?

    22 + ☐ = 30 and 40 – ☐ = 32

    (A) 10   (B) 8   (C) 18   (D) None of these

6. Which box contains a horizontal line?

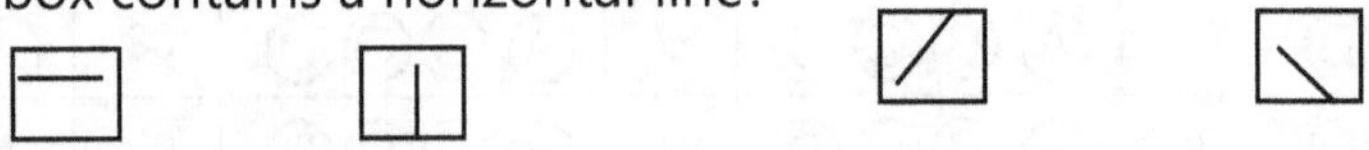

             A   B   C   D

    (A) A   (B) B   (C) C   (D) D

7. Which is less than 40 ?

   (A) | 10 | (B) | 50 | (C) | 100 | (D) | 50 | | 10 |

8. Which set of coins shows ₹ 5?

   (A) Two 50 paisa coins   (B) Five one rupee coins

   (C) Four 25 paisa coins   (D) Five ten paisa coins

9. ₹2 →  can be taken for

   (A) (25 P) (25 P) (25 P)   (B) (50 P) (50 P) (50 P) (50 P)

   (C) (₹ 1)   (D) None of these

10. Anushka wants to buy a toy for ₹ 45. She has ₹ 15. How much more money is needed?

    (A) 60   (B) 30   (C) 25   (D) None of these

11. Tanaya wants to exchange her ₹ 5 with some coins. Which set of coins can she use?

    (A) (50 P) (50 P) (50 P) (50 P) (₹ 2)

    (B) (50 P) (50 P) (25 P) (25 P) (25 P) (25 P)

    (C) (₹ 2) (₹ 1) (50 P) (50 P) (50 P) (50 P)

    (D) None of these

12. How much amount is shown?

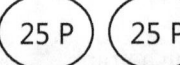 

(A) ₹ 68   (B) ₹ 128   (C) ₹ 68.50   (D) None of these

13. Which set of coins shows ₹ 3?

(A) (50 P) (50 P) (1)

(B) (25 P) (25 P) (25 P) (25 P) (₹ 1)

(C) (50 P) (50 P) (₹ 1) (₹ 1)

(C) None of these

14. Hrishika pays ₹ 90 for the  of ₹ 50 and _____

(A) 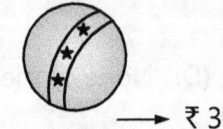 ⟶ ₹ 30

(B) 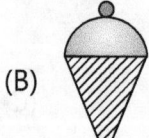 ⟶ ₹ 10

(C)  ⟶ ₹ 40

(D) None of these

15. ₹ 2 = ___

(A) Ten 10 paise coins   (B) Five 50 paise coins

(C) Four 25 paise coins   (D) Four 50 paise coins

16. 3 tens + 4 tens = _____

    (A) 30 tens   (B) 70 tens   (C) 7 tens   (D) 77 tens

17. Janhavi jumps 2 steps from 0 and then 3 steps. Where will she reach?

    1st Jump

    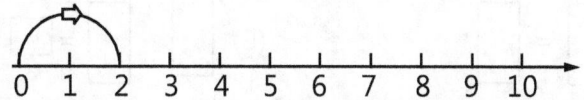

    (A) 2nd point   (B) 5th point

    (C) 3rd point   (D) None of these

18. 14 + 5 is shown by which abacus?

    (A)   (B)   (C)   (D) None of these

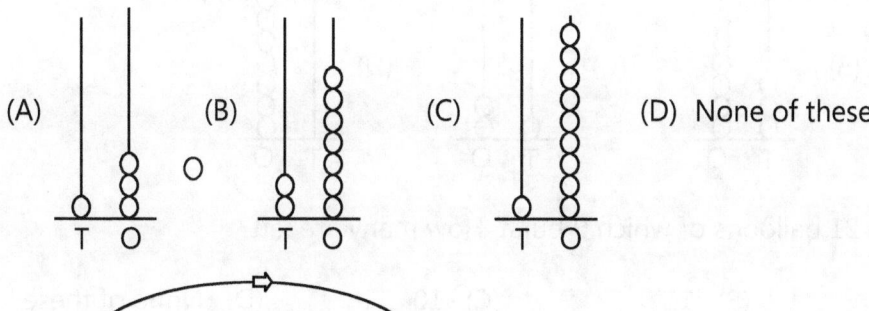

19.

The number line given represents which of the following?

    (A) 7 − 4 = 3   (B) 7 + 2 = 9

    (C) 7 − 3 = 4   (D) None of these

20. 8 tens - 4 tens 2 ones =

    (A) 33   (B) 40   (C) 38   (D) None of these

21. 6 tens 2 ones – 3 tens 9 ones =

    (A) 62   (B) 39   (C) 23   (D) None of these

22. 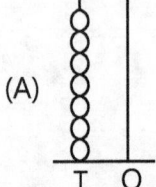 = 10 and ▢ = 5, which of the following is correct?

    (A) ☐ – ▯ = ▯   (B) ▯ – ▯ = ☐

    (C) ▯ – ☐ = ☐   (D) None of these

23. Which abacus shows 19 -12 = 7

(A)   (B)   (C)   (D)

    T O   T O   T O   T O

24. There are 21 balloons of which 9 burst. How many are left?

    (A) 12   (B) 11   (C) 10   (D) None of these

25. Take away 3 from 12 to give

    (A) 15   (B) 9   (C) 90   (D) None of these

26.

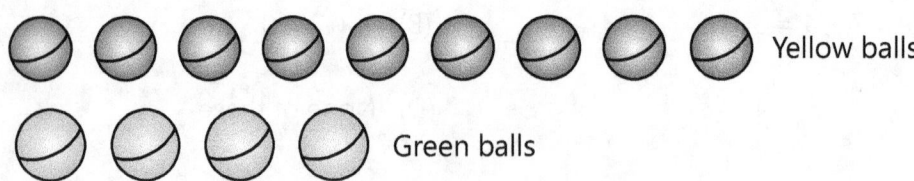

Yellow balls

Green balls

How many green balls are needed to make equal to yellow balls?

    (A) 5   (B) 3   (C) 8   (D) None of these

27. Which is same as 20 – 3?

(A) 14 – 4   (B) 30 – 23   (C) 25 – 8   (D) none of these

28.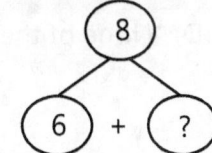

What will come in place of ?

(A) 14   (B) 2   (C) 3   (D) None of these

29. 4 more than 8 is represented by which number line?

(A)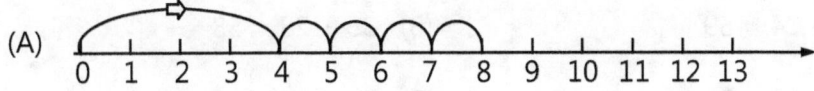

(B)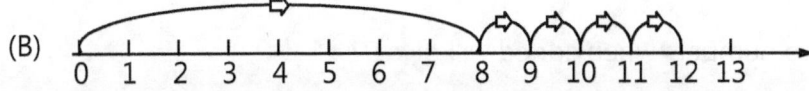

(C)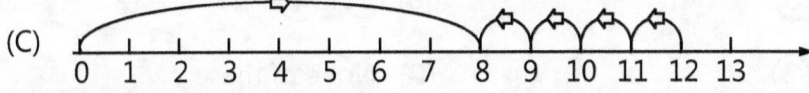

(D) None of these

30. 4 more than 33 + 14 is

(A) 47   (B) 51   (D) 37   (D) None of these

31. Rujuta has 26 sweets. Bhoomi gave her 11 more. Veda gave her 13 more. How many sweets does Rujuta have?

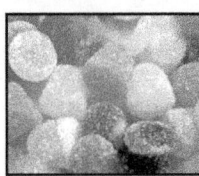

(A) 26 + 11 + 13   (B) 13 + 11 + 26

(C) Both a and b   (D)None of these

32. If I add this number to 14, I will get 17. What am I adding?

14 + ____ = 17

(A) 5   (B) 6   (C) 3   (D) None of these

33.

Which of the following does the abacus show?

(A) 35 + 24 = 59   (B) 35 + 23 = 58

(C) 34 + 25 = 59   (D) None of these

34. Which two numbers when added will give 9?

(A) ④+③   (B) ⑤+④

(C) ③+②   (D) None of these

35. A shopkeeper sold 23 dolls on Thursday. He sold 9 dolls less on Friday.

How many dolls are sold on Friday?

(A) 23 − 10 =13   (B) 23 + 9 = 31

(C) 23 − 9 = 14   (D) None of these

ANSWERSHEET

1.	Ⓐ Ⓑ Ⓒ Ⓓ	2.	Ⓐ Ⓑ Ⓒ Ⓓ	3.	Ⓐ Ⓑ Ⓒ Ⓓ	4.	Ⓐ Ⓑ Ⓒ Ⓓ
5.	Ⓐ Ⓑ Ⓒ Ⓓ	6.	Ⓐ Ⓑ Ⓒ Ⓓ	7.	Ⓐ Ⓑ Ⓒ Ⓓ	8.	Ⓐ Ⓑ Ⓒ Ⓓ
9.	Ⓐ Ⓑ Ⓒ Ⓓ	10.	Ⓐ Ⓑ Ⓒ Ⓓ	11.	Ⓐ Ⓑ Ⓒ Ⓓ	12.	Ⓐ Ⓑ Ⓒ Ⓓ
13.	Ⓐ Ⓑ Ⓒ Ⓓ	14.	Ⓐ Ⓑ Ⓒ Ⓓ	15.	Ⓐ Ⓑ Ⓒ Ⓓ	16.	Ⓐ Ⓑ Ⓒ Ⓓ
17.	Ⓐ Ⓑ Ⓒ Ⓓ	18.	Ⓐ Ⓑ Ⓒ Ⓓ	19.	Ⓐ Ⓑ Ⓒ Ⓓ	20.	Ⓐ Ⓑ Ⓒ Ⓓ
21.	Ⓐ Ⓑ Ⓒ Ⓓ	22.	Ⓐ Ⓑ Ⓒ Ⓓ	23.	Ⓐ Ⓑ Ⓒ Ⓓ	24.	Ⓐ Ⓑ Ⓒ Ⓓ
25.	Ⓐ Ⓑ Ⓒ Ⓓ	26.	Ⓐ Ⓑ Ⓒ Ⓓ	27.	Ⓐ Ⓑ Ⓒ Ⓓ	28.	Ⓐ Ⓑ Ⓒ Ⓓ
29.	Ⓐ Ⓑ Ⓒ Ⓓ	30.	Ⓐ Ⓑ Ⓒ Ⓓ	31.	Ⓐ Ⓑ Ⓒ Ⓓ	32.	Ⓐ Ⓑ Ⓒ Ⓓ
33.	Ⓐ Ⓑ Ⓒ Ⓓ	34.	Ⓐ Ⓑ Ⓒ Ⓓ	35.	Ⓐ Ⓑ Ⓒ Ⓓ	36.	Ⓐ Ⓑ Ⓒ Ⓓ
37.	Ⓐ Ⓑ Ⓒ Ⓓ	38.	Ⓐ Ⓑ Ⓒ Ⓓ	39.	Ⓐ Ⓑ Ⓒ Ⓓ	40.	Ⓐ Ⓑ Ⓒ Ⓓ
41.	Ⓐ Ⓑ Ⓒ Ⓓ	42.	Ⓐ Ⓑ Ⓒ Ⓓ	43.	Ⓐ Ⓑ Ⓒ Ⓓ	44.	Ⓐ Ⓑ Ⓒ Ⓓ
45.	Ⓐ Ⓑ Ⓒ Ⓓ	46.	Ⓐ Ⓑ Ⓒ Ⓓ	47.	Ⓐ Ⓑ Ⓒ Ⓓ	48.	Ⓐ Ⓑ Ⓒ Ⓓ
49.	Ⓐ Ⓑ Ⓒ Ⓓ	50.	Ⓐ Ⓑ Ⓒ Ⓓ	51.	Ⓐ Ⓑ Ⓒ Ⓓ	52.	Ⓐ Ⓑ Ⓒ Ⓓ
53.	Ⓐ Ⓑ Ⓒ Ⓓ	54.	Ⓐ Ⓑ Ⓒ Ⓓ	55.	Ⓐ Ⓑ Ⓒ Ⓓ	56.	Ⓐ Ⓑ Ⓒ Ⓓ
57.	Ⓐ Ⓑ Ⓒ Ⓓ	58.	Ⓐ Ⓑ Ⓒ Ⓓ	59.	Ⓐ Ⓑ Ⓒ Ⓓ	60.	Ⓐ Ⓑ Ⓒ Ⓓ
61.	Ⓐ Ⓑ Ⓒ Ⓓ	62.	Ⓐ Ⓑ Ⓒ Ⓓ	63.	Ⓐ Ⓑ Ⓒ Ⓓ	64.	Ⓐ Ⓑ Ⓒ Ⓓ
65.	Ⓐ Ⓑ Ⓒ Ⓓ	66.	Ⓐ Ⓑ Ⓒ Ⓓ	67.	Ⓐ Ⓑ Ⓒ Ⓓ	68.	Ⓐ Ⓑ Ⓒ Ⓓ
69.	Ⓐ Ⓑ Ⓒ Ⓓ	70.	Ⓐ Ⓑ Ⓒ Ⓓ	71.	Ⓐ Ⓑ Ⓒ Ⓓ	72.	Ⓐ Ⓑ Ⓒ Ⓓ
73.	Ⓐ Ⓑ Ⓒ Ⓓ	74.	Ⓐ Ⓑ Ⓒ Ⓓ	75.	Ⓐ Ⓑ Ⓒ Ⓓ	76.	Ⓐ Ⓑ Ⓒ Ⓓ
77.	Ⓐ Ⓑ Ⓒ Ⓓ	78.	Ⓐ Ⓑ Ⓒ Ⓓ	79.	Ⓐ Ⓑ Ⓒ Ⓓ	80.	Ⓐ Ⓑ Ⓒ Ⓓ
81.	Ⓐ Ⓑ Ⓒ Ⓓ	82.	Ⓐ Ⓑ Ⓒ Ⓓ	83.	Ⓐ Ⓑ Ⓒ Ⓓ	84.	Ⓐ Ⓑ Ⓒ Ⓓ
85.	Ⓐ Ⓑ Ⓒ Ⓓ	86.	Ⓐ Ⓑ Ⓒ Ⓓ	87.	Ⓐ Ⓑ Ⓒ Ⓓ	88.	Ⓐ Ⓑ Ⓒ Ⓓ
89.	Ⓐ Ⓑ Ⓒ Ⓓ	90.	Ⓐ Ⓑ Ⓒ Ⓓ	91.	Ⓐ Ⓑ Ⓒ Ⓓ	92.	Ⓐ Ⓑ Ⓒ Ⓓ
93.	Ⓐ Ⓑ Ⓒ Ⓓ	94.	Ⓐ Ⓑ Ⓒ Ⓓ	95.	Ⓐ Ⓑ Ⓒ Ⓓ	96.	Ⓐ Ⓑ Ⓒ Ⓓ
97.	Ⓐ Ⓑ Ⓒ Ⓓ	98.	Ⓐ Ⓑ Ⓒ Ⓓ	99.	Ⓐ Ⓑ Ⓒ Ⓓ	100.	Ⓐ Ⓑ Ⓒ Ⓓ

Answers

Chapter 1 : Number Sense

1. C. 82, 74, 56, 25.

    Descending order means arranging the numbers from the biggest number to smallest number.

2. B. 50

    50 comes after 49

3. B. 36

    $\qquad\qquad$ T $\quad$ O

    (3 tens) $\rightarrow$ 3 $\quad$ 6 $\leftarrow$ (6 ones)

4. C. 40. $\quad$ 40 comes between 39 and 41.

5. C. 80

    80 comes before 81.

6. B. 46. Forty-six

7. B. 33, 38, 83, 88

    Ascending order means arranging the numbers from small to big.

8. B. 90. After 89 comes 90.

9. C. 40+2

    40 + 2 = 42

    option a : 4+2 = 6 (incorrect)

    option b : 40-2=38 (incorrect)

    option d : 41-2=39 (incorrect)

10. B. 39.

    39 comes before 40.

11. D. Both b and C. 60-1= **59**, $\quad$ 50 + 9 = **59**

12. B. Balls are more than flowers.

    There are 5 balls and 3 flowers. So 2 more balls than flowers

13. C. There are no triangles in option C.

14. B. 98

      T   0

      9   8

15. B

Counting by 2' s means 2, 4, 6, 8

16. B. 74

17. B. 42.

Tens place has 4 beads and ones place has 2 beads.

18. D. Both the boxes have four dots.

19. C. 100

20. C.

1 more than 42 means 42+1=43. Option c shows 43 on abacus. 4 beads in tens place and 3 beads in ones place.

21. B. 29

1 less than 30 is 29.

30 − 1 = 29

22. C. 85, 72, 53, 49

Descending means big to small.

23. B. 70

Number has to be between 69 and 71. It is 70.

69   **70**   71.

24. D. 1 more than 29 means 29 + 1= 30. Option d shows 30 on abacus. 3 beads in tens place and 0 beads in ones place.

25. C. 51.

1 more than 50 is 50 + 1 = 51

26. C. 80.

Number between 79 and 8 1 is 80

79   **80**   81.

27. C . 21, 42, 68, 94

Option c numbers are arranged properly from small to big.

28. A. 83-1=82

29. C. 92.

30. A. 7 tens and 4 ones.

T   O

7   4.

7 in tens place and 4 in ones place.

31. B. 40.

40 comes after 39.

32. B. Triangles are less than ovals. There are 8 ovals and 5 triangles. 5 triangles are less than 8 ovals.

33. D. 79

79 comes before 80.

34. C.

Counting by 2' s means

2 + 2 = 4 + 2 = 6 + 2 = 8

Adding up 2 to each number. The first drop is on 2 next on 4 next on 6 next 8.

35. A. 80+9

80+9=89 option b) 89 + 9 = 98

option c) 70 + 9 =79

Both option b and c are incorrect.

36. C

1 more than 60 is 61 [60 + 1= 61].

Option a shows 5 beads in tens place and 6 beads in ones place = 56.

Option b shows 6 beads in tens place and 2 beads in ones place = 62.

Option c shows 6 beads in tens place and 1 bead in ones place = **61**.

37. B. 81, 24, 16, 3

38. B. 94

4 in ones place. 9 in tens place

T   O

9 4

39. B. 20 + 7

    7 ones means 7 in ones place =7

    2 tens means 2 in tens place =20

    T O

    2 7

40. B. 28

    8 ones means 8 in ones place = 8

    2 tens means 2 in tens place = 20

    T O

    2 8

41. D. 70

    Number between 69 and 71 is 70.

    69   **70**   71

42. B. 3 tens + 6 ones

    3 in tens place .6 in ones place.

    T O

    3 6

43. A. 72

    72 is the largest amongst 72, 27, 42, 09.

    09 means 9.

44. B. 80.

    8 tens means 8 in tens place. So nothing in ones place. Ones place zero (0) will be there

    T O

    8 O

45. C. 34

    3 tens means in 3 tens place.

    4 ones means 4 in ones place.

    T O

    3 4

46. D. 20

2 tens means 2 in tens place.

No number in ones place means, so we write there 0.

T O
2 0

47. B. 6 3

6 tens means 6 in tens place.

3 ones means 3 in ones place.

T O
6 3

48. B.27

7 in ones place, 2 in tens place So.

T O
2 7

49. C. 90

90 comes between 89 and 91

89 **90** 91

50. B. 37.

7 means 7 in ones place. 3 tens means 30

T O
3 7

Chapter 2 : Addition

1. C. 8 tens.

6 tens means   60
+ 2 tens means   + 20
                     80

Another way to write 80 is 8 tens.

Option A) 66 tens means 660 (wrong)

Option B) 80 tens means 800 (wrong)

Option C) 10 tens means 100 (wrong)

2. B. 93

90+ 3 = 93 OR 90
                + 3
                93

3. C.0.

   When you add 0 to any number, answer is that same number 40 + 0 = 40

4. C. 49

   3 more than 34 +12 means

   3 is added to the sum of 34+12

   So 34 + 12 + 3 = 49

5. C. 50+9

   option A   40 + 3 = 43

   option B   40 + 9 = 49

   option C   50 + 9 = 59   This is more or greatest.

   option D   40 + 8 = 48

6. D. 1

   81 + 1 = 82

   Only on adding 1 to 81 we get 82

7. B. 9 tens

   5 tens +4 tens ___

   $$5 \text{ tens} = 50$$
   $$+4\text{tens} = 40$$
   $$\overline{}$$
   $$90 \text{ means 9 tens.}$$

   Not 90 tens or 99 tens. Read carefully all the options.

8. B. 50

   36+14=50

9. B. 86.

   8 more than 78 is 86

   $$\begin{array}{r} 78 \\ +\ 8 \\ \hline 86 \end{array}$$

10. D. none of these

    18 more than 43+33 means add 18 to 42 + 33.

    Add 42 + 33 + 18 = 93.

    None of the options show 93.

11. B. 90

$$\begin{array}{r} 70 \\ +\ 20 \\ \hline 90 \end{array}$$

12. B. 12 + 5 = 17

Option (A) has one bead in tens place and 5 beads in ones place.

So the number is 15. We are in search of 17 (incorrect).

Option (B) has one bead in tens place and 7 beads in ones place. So the number is 17 (correct).

Option (C) has 2 beads in tens place and 1 bead in ones place. So the number 21 (incorrect).

Option (D) has no bead in tens place and 6 bead in ones place. The number is 6 (incorrect).

13. B. 6+3

On adding two numbers answer should be 9

Option a) 3 + 3 = 6 (incorrect)   Option b) **6 + 3 = 9** (correct)

Option)   9 + 3 = 12 (incorrect)   Option d) 2 + 4 = 6 (incorrect)

14. C. 50

Number of pencils Bhoomi has	46
Number of pencils she bought	+ 4
Altogether she has	50

15. C. 29.

There are 6 apples, 8 mangoes and 15 bananas.

$$\begin{array}{r} 6 \text{ apples} \\ +\ 8 \text{ mangoes} \\ +15 \text{ bananas} \\ \hline 29 \end{array}$$ Total number of fruits in the basket.

16. B. 3

Addition: 4+ which number will give the answer 7. 4 + **3** = 7

17. B. 5

Girl starts from 0. Her first jump is on 2 steps so she will come on number 2. Then she jumps 3 steps. So 2 + 3 = 5.

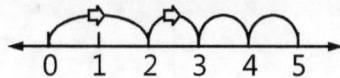

18. D. 6+6

On adding two numbers you should get 12

Option A) 6 + 4 = 10 (incorrect)

Option B) 4 + 3 = 7   (incorrect)

Option C) 9 + 2 = 11 (incorrect)

Option D) 6 + 6 = 12 (correct)

Only 6 + 6 will be 12.

19. B. 90.

It is an addition word problem.

Number of toys Ronit has	83
+ number of more toys he buys	+ 7
Number of toys Ronit has altogether	90

20. A. 49.

Number of elephants	18
Number of rabbits	+ 24
Number of tigers	+ 7
Total number of animals in the jungle	49

21. B. 7

11 plus which number will give 18.

11 + **7** = 18

22. B. 6

Kalu has 2 sticks	2
Ved has 4 sticks	+ 4
Total number of pencils	6

23. B. 41

It is addition word problem. (Keyword: in all)

Number of boys	14
Number of girls	+ 27
Number of students in class	41

24. A. 7

On adding a certain number to 23 you should get 30.

$23 + \_\_ = 30$

$23 + \underline{7} = 30$

25. B. 19

It is an addition word problem (Keyword: altogether)

Number of pens I have	9
Number of pens Raja gave me	+ 6
Number of pens Tina gave me	+ 4
Total number of pens I have.	19.

26. C. both A and B.

The first box has 7 balls, another box has 5 balls.

So 7 + 5 and 5 + 7 gives the same answer. Read all the options carefully (addition key word: in all)

27. B. 53+24=77

Count the number of bead in all three abacus carefully.

5 3   + 2 4   = 77

$$\begin{array}{r} 53 \\ + \ 24 \\ \hline 77 \end{array}$$

28. B. 60

Addition word problem (Keyword: altogether)

Number of books Dev has	48
Number of other books he buys	+ 12
Altogether he has	60 books.

29. B. 9

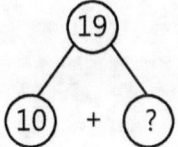

10 + 9 = 19

10 plus 9 will give you 19

30. C. 26+20

On adding which two numbers from the given options will you get 46.

Option A) 20 + 16 = 36

Option B) 26 + 40 = 66

Option C) 26 + 20 = 46.

31. B. 7th point.

Girl's first jump will take her to number 4. After 3 jumps she will be on number 7.

1st jump.

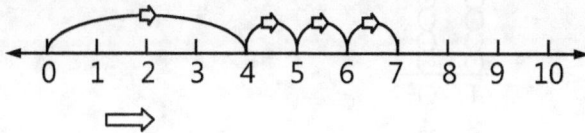

32. C. both A and B.

Addition word problem. Read the options carefully

Option A) 9+6+5 option B) 6 + 9 +5   option C) says both A and B.

33. A. 119

```
    62      (Addition).
+   57
───────
   119
```

34. C. 66

8 more than 17 + 41 means add 8 to 17 + 41. It means add 17 + 41 + 8 or else first add 17 + 41 and then add 8 to it.

```
        17          OR              17
     +  41                       +  41
     +   8                          58
        ───                      +   8
        66                          ───
                                    66
```

35. D. both A and C.

Read all the options carefully.

32 + 46 = _____

option A) 32+46 (correct)   option B) 46+36 (incorrect)

option C)46+32 (correct)   option D) both A and C.

36. D. 70+18

Option A) 60+7=67   option B) 30+14=44

Option C) 40+19=59   option D) 70+18=88 (greatest number).

37. A. 41+ 43=84

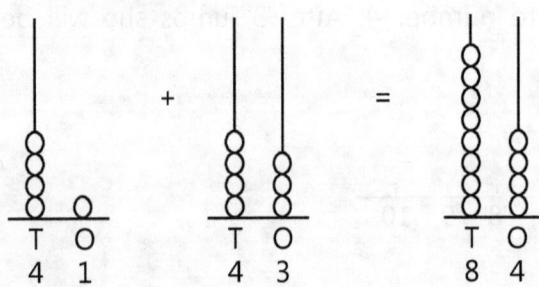

```
    T  O        T  O        T  O
    4  1        4  3        8  4
```

38.   D. 77

Addition word problem.

Number of dolls I have   28

+ Number of dolls Mona has   + 49

Total number of dolls   77

My dolls and Mona's dolls together is 77

39. A. 10 + 6

6 more than 10 means 10 + 6. Read all the options carefully.

40. A. 12 + 8

8 more than 12 is 12 + 8. Read the options carefully.

41. C. 5 more than 11 means 5+11=16. Only option c is showing 5 + 11 = 16.

    First jump on number 11 and then 5 more jumps. 11 + 5 = 16

42. D. 5 tens

3 tens means	30
+2 tens means	+20
	50

    50 means 5 tens. Read all the options carefully.

43. C. 7 tens

6 tens means	60
+1 tens means	+10
	70

    70 means 7 tens. Read all the options carefully.

44. A. 50 + 20 = 70

5 tens means	50
+2 tens means	+20
	70

    70 means 7 tens. Read all the options carefully.

45. B.

    4 more than 8 is represented as 4 + 8 = 12 OR 8 + 4 = 12.

     Study all the number lines carefully. Option B says 8 + 4 = 12. First jump on 8 and then 4 steps

46. D. 81.

Number of boys	42
Number of girls	+ 39
Total number of students in the class.	81

    (addition word problem).

47. B. 9+10

    On adding which two numbers from the given options will you get 19.

    Option A) 41 + 14 = 55.

Option B) 9 + 10 = **19** (correct)

Option C) 16 + 21 = 37

48. D. 40.

Addition word problem.

Number of toys I have	14
Number of toys my friend gave me	+ 26
Total number of toys I have	40

49. D. both B and C

Number of people in one bus = 39

Number of people in another bus = 48

Number of people in two buses = 39 + 48 OR 48 + 39

50. B. 59

$$
\begin{array}{r}
29 \\
+\ 30 \\
\hline
59
\end{array}
$$

Chapter 3 : Subtraction

1. B. 8

Subtraction word problem

Total number of balls in a basket	10
Number of balls taken away.	– 2
Number of balls in the basket.	8

2. A. 15- 3 = 12

Here, butterflies flew away. So we subtract.

Number of butterflies	15
Number of butterflies flew away	– 3
Number of butterflies left	12

Read the options carefully

Option A) 15 – 3 = 12   (Correct)

Option B) 3 – 15 = 12 (Incorrect)

Option C) 13 – 5 = 8 (Incorrect)

3.   B.   19 – 7 = 12

Raj ate 7 chocolates from 19. Means 7 chocolates less.   When something becomes less from the total collection we subtract.

Read all the options carefully

Option A) 17 – 9 = 12 (Incorrect)

Option B) 19 – 7 = 12 (Correct)

Option C) 7 – 19 = 12 (Incorrect)

4.   A. 19-8=11

8 less than 19 means 19 - 8 (8 less).

19 – 8 = 11

Read all the options carefully.

Option A) 19 – 8 = 11 (Correct)

Option B) 19 – 11 = 8 (Incorrect)

Option C) 11 – 8 = 2 (Incorrect)

Option D) 11 + 8 = 9 (Incorrect)

5.   B.

Big oval's value $\bigcirc$ = 20

Small oval's value $\bigcirc$ = 10

It means big oval 20 $\bigcirc$ - small oval 10 $\bigcirc$ = small oval 10 $\bigcirc$

$\bigcirc$ – $\bigcirc$ = $\bigcirc$

  20   –   10   =   10

Place the values and solve.

6.   B. 6.

Take away 3 from 9 means 9 – 3 = 6

Remember. You cannot do 3 - 9. Always smaller number is subtracted from a greater number.

7.   D. ☐ – ☐ = ☐

Big rectangle ☐ = 28, small rectangle ☐ = 14

☐ – ☐ = ☐

28   – 14 = 14

Place the values and solve. Option d is showing the correct value.

8.   A. $36 - 9 = 27$

9 less than 36 means $36 - 9 = 27$

Read all the options carefully.

9.   A. 66

$$\begin{array}{r} 93 \\ -\ 27 \\ \hline 66 \end{array}$$

10. A. 18

Subtraction word problem.

Number of balloons	32
Number of balloons bursted	– 14
Number of balloons left.	18

Keywords for subtraction: how many left , how many more, how many less, difference.

11. B. $10 - 5$

$14 - 9$

$$\begin{array}{r} 14 \\ -\ 9 \\ \hline 5 \end{array}$$

You have to search for an option which will give you 5.

option A)   15-3=12 (incorrect)

option B) 10-5 = ☐5 (correct)

option C) 14-4=10 (incorrect)

12. B. 5

12 – 5 = 7   means from the total 12 balls remove or cross out 5 balls.

13. B. 6 – 4 = 2

Subtraction word problem.

Rishu has	6	ice creams
She gave away	– 4	ice creams
	2	

14. D. 7.

Total number of arrows	9
less	– 2
	7

15. C. 52

8 tens 4 ones	=	84
3 tens 2 ones	=	– 32
		52

16. A. 14 – 6 = 8

Read all the options carefully.

Number of pens Riya has	14
– Number of pens she gave to Mona	– 6
Number of pens left	8

option A) 14 – 6 = 8   (correct)

option B) 16 – 4 = 12 (incorrect)

option C) 14 – 8 = 6   (incorrect)

17. D. 8.

Subtraction word problem

When you remove something from the collection you have to subtract.

Number of bugs	22
Number of bugs went away	– 14
Number of bugs left	8

18. B. 2.

    Subtraction word problem

    Count the ice- creams properly

Number of ice-creams	6
Number of ice-creams melt	− 4
Number of ice-creams left	2

19. D. 40 − 24 = 16.

    30 − 14 = 16

    We have to search for an option which will give you 16.

    Option A) 36 − 14 = 22 (incorrect)

    Option B) 24 − 10 = 14 (incorrect)

    Option C) 40 − 30 = 10 (incorrect)

    Option D) 40 − 24 = 16 (correct)

20. B. 6.

      Green ovals

    Red ovals

    Count the ovals carefully.

    There are 10 green ovals.

    There are 4 red ovals.

    We need 6 more red ovals to make it equal to green ovals.

21. B. 4.

    9 − 5 dots means 9 − 5 = 4

    5 dots represent number 5.

22. A .67

    96 − 29 = 67   (subtraction burrowing)

23. C. 89 − 39 = 50

Read all the options carefully.

8 tens 9 ones = 89

3 tens 9 ones = $-$ 39
$$\overline{50}$$

89 − 39 = 50

24. B. 8 − 3 = 5

Subtraction on number line

25. B. 24

Subtraction word problem

Number of dolls sold on Wednesday   28

4 dolls less sold on Thursday.   − $\underline{4}$

  Number of dolls sold on Thursday   24

26. C. 27 − 14 = 13

Observe and count the beads of abacus carefully. Search for an abacus which shows number 13.

27. B. 36.

Take away 12 means subtract 12 from 48.

48 − 12 = 36.

28. B. 30 − 16.

Option A) 30 − 6 = 24

Option B) 32 − 18 = 14

Option C) 26 − 10 = 16

Option D) 48 − 13 = 35.

14 is the least number.

29. A. 50 − 12 = 38

Number of sweets Bhoomi has   50

Number of sweets she ate   − $\underline{12}$

Number of sweets left.   38

Read all the options carefully.

30. D. 63 – 13 = 50

Observe and count the beads of all the abacus carefully. Search for an abacus which shows number 50.

Option D) Tens place 5 beads so 5 tens and ones place 0 beads

T O

5 0

31. C. 5 tens

8 tens means   80

3 tens means   – 30

50

Read all the options carefully.

32. D. none of these

9 tens means   90

6 tens means   – 60

30   OR   3 tens

33. A.   4 tens 1 ones

T O

7 tens 4 ones   7 4

3 tens 3 ones   –   3 3

4 1

41 means 4 tens 1 ones.

Read all the options carefully.

34. B. 9 – 2 = 7

There are 9 ovals in all. 2 ovals crossed out So. 9 – 2 = 7.

35. A. 7.

12 minus 5 dots means 12 – 5 = 7

36. B. 6.

To show 14 – 6 = 8, cross out 6 circles. (– 6 means less 6 or take away 6)

37. A. 32 – 19 = 13

19 less than 32 means 32 – 19 = 13

38. A.

big rectangle ▯ = 20

small square ☐ = 10

Put the value of rectangles and squares.

option A)

▯ – ☐ = ☐

20 – 10 = 10

39. B.

32 – 10 = 22

Search for an abacus which shows number 22

40. A. 10 – 3 = 7

The number line shows 10 – 3 = 7. First step on 10 and then backwards 3 steps.

41. A. 48 – 8 = 40.

Number of dolls sold on Saturday   48.

Number of less dolls sold on Sunday   – 8

Number of dolls sold on Sunday   40

42. B. 39 – 4 = 35

Number of pencils sold in January   39

Number of pencils less sold in February   –   4

Number of pencils sold in February   35

43. C. 4

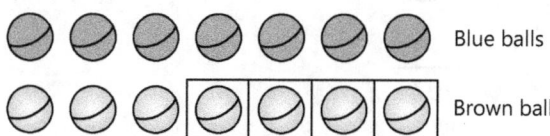

Blue balls

Brown balls

Count the balls carefully

Number of blue balls   = 7

Number of brown balls   = 3

We need 4 more brown balls to make it equal to blue balls.

44. A. 22.

Take away 6 means subtract 6 from 28

28 – 6 = 22

45. B. 30.

Take away 19 means subtract 19 from 49.

49 – 19 = 30.

46. A. 17

Number of balloons	49
Number of balloons blown away	– 32
Number of balloons left	17

47. D.2

5 – 3 = 2. Count carefully.

48. A. 21

Subtraction word problem

Number of dolls Kuhu has	57
Number of dolls she gave her sister	– 36
Number of dolls left with Kuhu	21

49. B. 7

Subtraction word problem. Read the question carefully.

13 biscuits eaten from the packet of 20

Number of biscuits	20
Number of biscuits Raja ate	– 13
Number of biscuits left	07

50. B. 2 tens

9 tens means	90
7 tens means	– 70
	20 (2 tens)

Chapter 4 : Money

1. A. ₹ 2 + ₹ 2

    2 + 2 = 4

2. B. ₹ 100

    Cost of the ball is 60 ₹. To buy it we need either ₹ 60 or more than 60.

    ₹ 100 is more than ₹ 60.

3. B. ₹ 65

    ₹ 10 + ₹ 50 + ₹ 5

    $$\begin{array}{r} 10 \\ + \ 50 \\ + \ \ 5 \\ \hline 65 \end{array}$$

4. B. ₹ 32

    ₹ 10 + ₹ 20 + ₹ 2 = ₹ 32

    $$\begin{array}{r} 10 \\ + \ 20 \\ + \ \ 2 \\ \hline 32 \end{array}$$

5. C. ₹ 2, Rs I, ₹ 5.

    Count the money carefully.

    Option a) ₹ 2 +₹ 2 + ₹ 2 =₹ 6

    Option b) ₹ 5 + ₹ 5 = ₹ 10.

    Option c) ₹ 2 + ₹ 1 + ₹ 5 = ₹ 8

6. C. ₹ 20.

    Cost of the balloon is ₹ 10. We need either ₹ 10 or more than that

    ₹ 2, ₹ 5, ₹ 1 is less than ₹ 10. ₹20 is more than ₹ 10.

7. B. ₹ 15.

    Cost of the mango is ₹ 15.

    ₹ 5, ₹ 10, ₹ 2 is less than ₹ 15. We need ₹ 15 to buy it.

8. A. 20

    Cost of one pencil is ₹ 10. Cost of two pencils will be 10 + 10 = 20.

9. C. ₹ 30.

    Rita has ₹ 50. She can buy items which are either equal to ₹ 50 or less than ₹ 50

    Option C) toy is for ₹ 30 which is less than ₹ 50.

10. A. Four 50 paisa coins.

    Option A) Four 50 paisa coins means 4 coins of 50 paisa.

$$
\begin{array}{r}
50\ p \\
+\ 50\ p \\
+\ 50\ p \\
+\ 50\ p \\
\hline
200\ \ p = ₹\ 2
\end{array}
$$

    200 p is ₹ 2

    Option B) five 50 paisa coins means 5 coins of 50 paisa.

$$
\begin{array}{r}
50\ p \\
+\ 50\ p \\
+\ 50\ p \\
+\ 50\ p \\
+\ 50\ p \\
\hline
250\ p = ₹\ \ 2.50
\end{array}
$$

    250 p is not ₹ 2

    Option C) four 10 paisa coins means 4 coins of 10 paisa.

$$
\begin{array}{r}
10\ p \\
+\ 10\ p \\
+\ 10\ p \\
+\ 10\ p \\
\hline
40\ p\ \text{is not}\ ₹\ 2
\end{array}
$$

    Option D) Ten 10 paisa coins means 10 coins of 10 paisa which is 100 p = Re 1 (not ₹ 2)

11. B. 300

    ₹ 3 = 300 p

12. C. 500

    ₹ 5 = 500 p

13. A. 800

    ₹ 8 = 800 p

14. C. Two 50 paisa coins

    Option A) Two 10 paisa coins means 2 coins of 10 paisa

    $$10 \text{ p}$$
    $$+ \ 10 \text{ p}$$
    $$20 \text{ P} \text{ is not } 1 ₹ \text{ (incorrect option)}$$

    Option B) Four 20 paisa coins means 4 coins of 20 paisa

    $$20 \text{ p}$$
    $$20 \text{ p}$$
    $$20 \text{ p}$$
    $$+ \ 20 \text{ p}$$
    $$80 \text{ P} \text{ is not } 1 ₹ \text{ (incorrect option)}$$

    Option C) Two 50 paisa coins means 2 coins of 50 paisa

    $$50 \text{ p}$$
    $$+ \ 50 \text{ p}$$
    $$100 \text{ P} = 1 ₹ \text{ (correct option)}$$

    Option D) Five 25 paisa coins means 5 coins of 25 paisa

    $$25 \text{ p}$$
    $$25 \text{ p}$$
    $$25 \text{ p}$$
    $$25 \text{ p}$$
    $$+ \ 25 \text{ p}$$
    $$125 \text{ P} \text{ is not } 1 ₹ \text{ (incorrect option)}$$

15. B. Five one rupee coins.

   ₹ 5 = 500 p

   Which option is giving the total of ₹ 5 or 500 p.

   Option A) Four 50 paisa coins means four coins of 50 paisa.

   50 p + 50 p + 50 p + 50 p = 200 p = 2 rupees (incorrect option)

   Option B) Five 1 rupee coins means 5 coins of one rupee.

   ₹ 1 + ₹ 1 + ₹ 1 + ₹ 1 + ₹ 1 = ₹ 5 (Correct)

   Option C) Five 10 paisa coins means 5 coins of 10p

   10 p + 10 p + 10 p + 10 p + 10 p = 50 p (incorrect)

16. C. Eight 50 p coins.

   Search for an option which will give you ₹ 4 or 400 P.

   Option A) Four 10 paisa coins means four coins of 10 paisa.

   10 + 10 + 10 + 10 = 40p (incorrect option)

   Option B) Five 50 p coins means five coins of 50 paisa.

   50 p + 50 p + 50 p + 50p + 50 p = 250p (incorrect option)

   Option C) Eight 50 paisa means eight coins of 50 paisa.

   50 p + 50 p + 50 p + 50p + 50 p + 50 p + 50p + 50 p = 400 p = 4 ₹

   ANOTHER WAY

   2 coins of 50 p = 1 ₹
   2 coins of 50 p = 1 ₹
   2 coins of 50 p = 1 ₹
   2 coins of 50 p = 1 ₹
   _____
   8 coins of 50 p   4 ₹ = 400 p

17. D. 700

   ₹ 7 = 700 P

18. B. 15

Cost of one book   ₹ 5

So cost of 3 books will be ₹ 5 + ₹ 5 + ₹ 5 = ₹ 15

Cost of first book   ₹ 5

Cost of second book   +   ₹ 5

Cost of third book   +   ₹ 5
                                        ─────
                                        ₹ 15

Mona needs ₹ 15 for 3 books.

19. C. 170

$$
\begin{array}{r}
10 \\
+\ 10 \\
+\ 50 \\
+\ 100 \\
\hline
170
\end{array}
$$

20. B. 175

$$
\begin{array}{r}
₹\ 100 \\
+\ ₹\ \ 50 \\
+\ ₹\ \ 20 \\
+\ ₹\ \ \ \ 5 \\
\hline
₹\ 175
\end{array}
$$

21. A.

With ₹ 50 Raju can buy articles which costs less than 50. Only star cost less than 50 ₹. Star is for 30 ₹.

22) C.

With ₹ 80 Mohan can buy items worth ₹ 80 or less than ₹ 80. Only option c balloon costs less than ₹ 80. It costs ₹ 70.

23. B. 3

Cost of one ball is ₹ 10 . For 30 ₹ Rahul can buy 3 balls.

1st ball ₹ 10

+ 2nd ball ₹ 10

+ 3rd ball ₹ 10

₹ 30

24. A. 4

Cost of one ball is ₹ 10

If he buys 1st ball   ₹ 10

If he buys 2st ball   +   ₹ 10 (= 20)

If he buys 3rd ball   +   ₹ 10 (= 30)

If he buys 4th ball   +   ₹ 10

₹ 40

With ₹ 40 Raj can buy 4 balls.

25. C. ₹ 1, ₹ 2, 50 p, 50 p.

From the four options we have to search, which set of money shows ₹ 4.

Option A)   ₹ 1

                         ₹ 1

                         ₹ 1 (50 p + 50 p)

                         ₹ 3 (incorrect)

Option B)   ₹ 2

                         ₹ 2

                         ₹ 1 (50 p + 50 p)

                         ₹ 5 (incorrect)

Option C)   ₹ 1

                         ₹ 2

                         ₹ 1 (50 p + 50 p)

                         ₹ 4 (correct)

Option D)   ₹ 1

                         ₹ 2

                         ₹ 2

                         ₹ 5 (incorrect)

26. D. 2

Cost of one toy car is ₹ 5.

Mehul can buy 2 toy cars with ₹ 10.

1st toy car		₹	5
2nd toy car	+	₹	5
		₹	10

So with ₹ 10 he can buy 2 toy cars.

27. B. ₹ 2, ₹ 2, 50 p, 50 p.

From the given options we have to search for a set of money which shows ₹ 5.

Option A)   ₹ 2

₹ 1

₹ 1 (50 p + 50 p)

₹ 4 (incorrect)

Option B)   ₹ 2

₹ 2

₹ 1 (50 p + 50 p)

₹ 5 (correct)

Option C)   ₹ 1

₹ 1

₹ 1 (50 p + 50 p)

₹ 3 (incorrect)

28. C. ₹ 52 and 50 p

Add rupees separately and 50 p separately.

₹ 1

+ ₹ 1

+ ₹ 52

₹ 52 + 50 p.

So ₹ 52 and 50 p

29. B. ₹ 24 and 50 p

Separate rupees and paisa.

₹ 10

$$
\begin{aligned}
+ \quad & ₹ \ 10 \\
+ \quad & ₹ \ 2 \\
+ \quad & ₹ \ 2 \\
\hline
& ₹ \ 24 \ + 50 \ p
\end{aligned}
$$

So ₹ 24 and 50 P.

30. A. ₹ 73 and 50 p. Separate rupees and paisa.

$$
\begin{aligned}
& ₹ \ 50 \\
+ \quad & ₹ \ 10 \\
+ \quad & ₹ \ 10 \\
+ \quad & ₹ \ 2 \\
+ \quad & ₹ \ 1 \\
\hline
& ₹ \quad 73 \ + 50 \ p
\end{aligned}
$$

So ₹ 73 and 50 P.

31. B.   ice-cream cone   ◄——— ₹ 20

Meena pays ₹ 50 for a mango of ₹ 30 and ice-cream worth ₹ 20. Read the question carefully. They are saying Meena has bought two items, one is mango of ₹ 30 and which is the other item. (she bought two items for ₹ 50). From ₹ 50 she spent ₹ 30. So 20 ₹ are left with her.

$$
\begin{aligned}
& ₹ \ 50 \\
- \quad & ₹ \ 30 \\
\hline
& ₹ \ 20
\end{aligned}
$$

Now with this ₹ 20 she has bought another item that costs ₹ 20. Only ice-cream costs ₹ 20.

32. C.   ← | ₹ 40 |

Read the question carefully. Ved pays ₹ 60 for the △ of ₹ 20 and which other item? (he bought 2 items for ₹ 60). From the total ₹ 60 he spent ₹ 20. So now 40 ₹ are left. 60 – 20 = 40.

Which item costs ₹ 40 ?

Only ice-cream costs ₹ 40.

33. C . ₹ 20

Read the question carefully.

It says Rita pays ₹ 50 for a)) of ₹ 30 and which other item. (She bought two items) Two items together cost ₹ 50.

From ₹ 50 she spent ₹ 30

$$\begin{array}{r} 50 \\ - \; 30 \\ \hline 20 \end{array}$$

Now ₹ 20 is left with her. Option C. ice cream costs ₹ 20.

34. B. ₹ 23 and 50 p.

First add only rupees and then paisa.

$$\begin{array}{r} ₹ \quad 1 \\ ₹ \quad 2 \\ ₹ 20 \\ \hline ₹ 23 + 50 \; p \end{array}$$

So ₹ 23 and 50 P.

35. A. 3

Cost of one toy car is ₹ 10. He has ₹ 35.

If he buys one car he has to pay ₹ 10.

If he buy two cars he has to pay 10 + 10 = ₹ 20, he will be left with some money. So he can buy one more car.

Then for 3rd toy cars he has to pay 10+10 + 10 = 30 ₹.

Still he is left with some money.

Let's see if he can buy one more car (4th car) 10 + 10 + 10 + 10 = 40.

He cannot buy 4 cars because it will cost ₹ 40 which is more than ₹ 35.

So he can buy only 3 cars.

       1st car   10
       2nd car   10
       3rd car   10
       _____
       ₹ 30

36. C. 2

Cost of one ice-creams ₹ 20. With ₹ 50, Mona can buy how many ice-creams ?
If she buys one ice-cream she has to pay ₹ 20. Still she is left with money
50 – 20 = 30 ₹.

She can buy one more ice-cream of ₹ 20.

30 – 20 = 10 ₹.

She still has ₹ 10, but cost of ice-cream is ₹ 20 so she can't buy the 3rd ice-cream .

1st ice-cream   = ₹ 20
2nd ice-cream   = ₹ 20
                    _____
                     ₹ 40

With ₹ 50 she can buy 2 ice-creams.

37. A. ₹ 1, ₹ 1, 50 p, 50 p.

Add rupees separately and paisa separately

Option A)   ₹ 1
                  + ₹ 1
                  + ₹ 1 (50 p + 50 p)
                  _____
                     ₹ **3**   (correct)

Option B)   ₹ 2
                     ₹ 2
                  _____
                     ₹ 4 and 50 p   (incorrect)

Option C)   ₹ 1

              ₹ 2

              ₹ 3 and 50 p (incorrect)

Option D)   ₹ 2

              ₹ 1

              ₹ 3 and 50p (incorrect)

38. D. None of these.

Search for an option which shows ₹ 6.

Option A)   ₹ 2

              ₹ 1

              ₹ 2

              ₹ 5 and 50 p (incorrect)

Option B)   ₹ 2

              ₹ 2

              ₹ 1

              ₹ 1

              ₹ 1 (50 p + 50 p)

              ₹ 7 (incorrect)

Option C)   ₹ 2

              ₹ 2

              ₹ 2

              ₹ 2

              ₹ 8 (incorrect)

39. B. 50 p, 50 p

Cost of one balloon is ₹ 1.

Which set of money will give you one rupee?

Option a)

         1 rupee (50 p + 50 p)

    +   1 rupee

          2 rupees   (incorrect)

Option B)   50 p

        + 50 p

        100 p = 1 Rupee (correct)

Option C)   1 ₹

          + 1 ₹

          + 2 ₹

          + 2 ₹

          ₹ 6 (incorrect)

Option D)   ₹ 2

        + ₹ 1

        ₹ 3 + 50 p (incorrect)

40. C. Six 50 paisa coins.

   ₹ 3 = 300 p.

   Search for an option which gives us 300p OR ₹ 3. Read the options carefully.

   Option A) Four 50 paisa coins means 4 coins of 50 paisa.

          50 p + 50 p + 50 p + 50 p = 200 p = 2 ₹ (incorrect)

   Option B) Three 50 paisa coins means 3 coins of 50p.

          50 p + 50 p + 50 p = 150 p (incorrect)

   Option C) Six 50 paisa means 6 coins of 50 paisa.

          50 p + 50 p + 50 p + 50 p + 50 p + 50 p = 300 p =3 ₹ (correct)

   Another way : Two 50p   will make 1 Rupee

   50p + 50 p = 1 Rupee

   50p + 50 p = 1 Rupee

   50p + 50 p = 1 Rupee

          3 Rupees (correct)

   Option D) Two 25 paisa coins means two coins of 25 paisa

   25 p + 25 p = 50 p.

41. B. ₹ 1, ₹ 2, ₹ 2

   Cost of the toy aeroplane is ₹ 5

   Search for a set of money which will give you ₹ 5

Option A)   50 p

        + 50 p

        + 50 p

        ————

       150 p (incorrect)

Option B)   ₹ 1

        ₹ 2

        ₹ 2

        ————

       ₹ 5 (correct)

Option C)   50 p

        + 50 p

        + 50 p

        + 50 p

        ————

       200 p = 2 ₹ (incorrect)

42. C. ₹ 2

Cost of the 2 toy phones is ₹ 8.

Soham gave ₹ 10 to buy the phones to the shopkeeper. ₹ 10 is more than ₹ 8. He gave extra or more money to the shopkeeper.

$$\begin{array}{r} 10 \\ -\ 8 \\ \hline 2\ ₹ \end{array}$$

The shopkeeper will return him ₹ 2.

Soham will get back ₹ 2.

43. D. ₹ 7

Cost of the toy is ₹ 13.   Rita gave more money. She gave ₹ 20 to the shopkeeper. So she will get back the more or extra money that is given to the shopkeeper.

$$\begin{array}{r} 20 \\ -\ 13 \\ \hline 7 \end{array}$$

She will get back ₹ 7.

44. B. 25p, 25 p, 25 p, 25 p

Sam wants to exchange his 1 rupee with some coins. We have to search for a set of money that will give us Rupee 1 or 100 P.

Option A) Rupee 1 + Rupee 1 = ₹ 2 (incorrect)

Option B) 25 p + 25 p + 25 p + 25 p = 100 p = 1 Rupee (correct)

Option C) 50p + 50 p + 50 p + 50 p = 200 p = ₹ 2 (incorrect)

Option D) Rupee 1 and 50 p (incorrect)

45. C. 50 p, 50 p, 50 p

Sania wants to exchange ₹ 2 with some coins. We have to search for a set of coins that will give us ₹ 2 or 200 p.

Option A)   50 p

          + 50 p

          100 p = Rupee 1 (incorrect)

Option B)   25 p

          + 25 p

          + 25 p

          + 25 p

          100 p = 1 Rupee (incorrect)

Option C)   50 p

          + 50 p

          + 50 p

          + 50 p

          200 p = ₹ 2 (correct)

46. C.

₹ 230, ₹ 123, ₹ 250, ₹ 97

₹ 250 is the greatest.

47. D.

₹ 146, ₹ 264, ₹ 210, ₹ 120

₹ 120 is the least.

48. C ₹ 20 + ₹ 50

    Option A)   ₹ 80

                    + ₹ 30
    _____

                    ₹ 110   (greater than ₹ 90)

    Option B) ₹ 100 is greater than ₹ 90.

    Option C)   ₹ 20

                    + ₹ 50
    _____

                    ₹ 70   less than ₹ 90 (correct)

    Option D) ₹ 150 is greater than ₹ 90.

49. A. 48

    Option A) ₹ 48 is less than ₹ 70 (correct)

    Option B)   ₹ 50

                    + ₹ 40
    _____

                    + ₹ 90   greater than ₹ 70 (incorrect) .

    Option C)   ₹ 30

                    + ₹ 50
    _____

                    + ₹ 80   greater than ₹ 70 (incorrect) .

    Option D) ₹ 90 is greater than ₹ 70 (incorrect).

50. B. ₹ 20

    Cost of the ball is ₹ 30.

    Sonu gave ₹ 50. She gave more money. So she will get back extra or more money.

                    ₹ 50

                    ₹ 30
    _____

                    ₹ 20

    She will get back 20 ₹.

51. D. ₹ 9

    Cost of the star is ₹ 11.

    Sham gave ₹ 20 to buy this star. He gave more money. So he will get back the extra, more money.

$$₹ 20$$
$$₹ 11$$
$$\overline{}$$
$$₹ \ 9$$

She will get back ₹ 9.

52. C. ₹ 5

Cost of an ice-cream is ₹ 15. Radha wants to buy it but she has only ₹ 10. She needs more money.

$$₹ 15$$
$$- ₹ 10$$
$$\overline{}$$
$$₹ \ 5$$

She needs ₹ 5 more to buy this ice-cream.

Let's check. ₹ 10 + ₹ 5 = ₹ 15.

53. C. ₹ 15

Cost of the mango is ₹ 75.

Rita has ₹ 60. She needs more money to buy it.

$$₹ 75$$
$$- ₹ 60$$
$$\overline{}$$
$$₹ 15$$

She needs ₹ 15 more to buy it.

Let's check. ₹ 60 + ₹ 15 = ₹ 75.

54. B.

Read the question carefully .

Roy pays ₹ 90 for toy aeroplane of ₹ 50 and one more item. (He bought two items for ₹ 90).

From ₹ 90 he spent ₹ 50 for toy aeroplane.

$$90$$
$$- 50$$
$$\overline{}$$
$$40$$

Now ₹ 40 is left with him.

Option B)  is for ₹ 40

55. A. 2

Cost of one book is ₹ 30.

If he buys one more book he needs.

30 + 30 = 60 ₹

Then he is left with ₹ 10. He cannot buy the third book with 10 ₹.

56. D. 60.

Cost of one bag is ₹ 20.

Tom bought 3 bags . So he has to pay

$$
\begin{array}{r}
₹\ 20 \\
+\quad ₹\ 20 \\
+\quad ₹\ 20 \\
\hline
₹\ 60 \\
\end{array}
$$

Chapter 5 : Geometry

1. D. Rohan

Rohan is on the top.

2. A. Ram

Ram is standing at the bottom.

3. D. Rohan

Rohan is standing above Sonu.

4. A. Ram

Ram is standing below Ritu.

5. A.

6. B.

Opposite sides of a rectangle are equal.

7. A. 6

Count only the circles carefully.

8. A.

Shaded part is a rectangle. Opposite sides of a rectangle are equal.

9. C. 10

Count the triangles carefully.

10. A. Cube.

In the given figure cone, cylinder and sphere is there. Only cube is not given.

11. C. Three

A triangle has 3 sides and 3 corners.

12. A. Triangle

In the given figure square, rectangle and circle is there. Only triangle is not shown there.

13. D. 5

One big triangle and four triangles inside.

14. A. Oval

15. C.

Box C contains all ovals.

16. B. 4.

Chapter 6 : Logical and Analytical Reasoning

1. C. ◯

| Square | triangle | square | oval | square | triangle | square | oval |

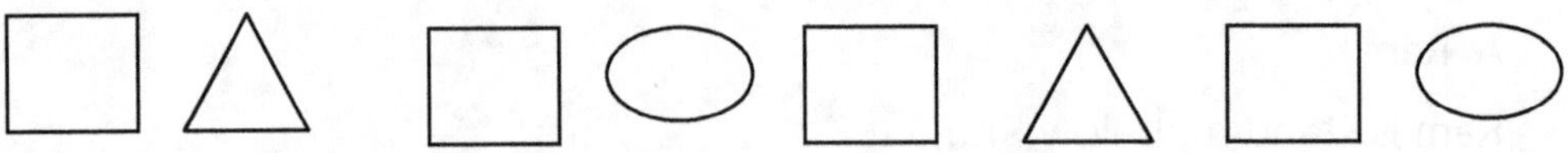

2. B. 30

Add 5 to each number is the rule.

| +5 | +5 | +5 | +5 | + 5 |
| 5 | 10 | 15 | 20 | 25 |

OR 5 times table.

3. A.

Cone   rectangle cone   oval   cone   rectangle   cone   oval

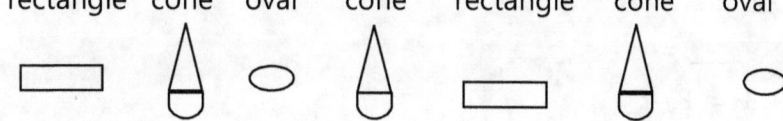

4. D. P

Last ice-cream is L. So first will be P.

5. A.

Observe the pattern carefully.

6. B. J

Observe carefully.

1st ball is E.

5th ball is I. I is before J.

7. B.

Observe the figure carefully.

8. B. 5

△ means '+' sign

▽ means '−' sign

So now 5 △ 5 means 5 + 5 (Replace △ with + sign)

And 15 ▽ __ means 15 − __ (Replace ▽ with − sign)

$$5 + 5 = 15 - \underline{\quad}$$
$$10 = 15 - \underline{\quad}$$
$$10 = 15 - \boxed{5}$$
$$10 = 10$$

Number on the left hand side of the equal to sign and right hand side of the equal to sign should be same after solving.

9. C. 3

△   Means   +

▽   Means   −

Now replace it with signs

$2 \triangle 3 = 2 + 3$

$8 \triangledown \underline{} = 8 - \underline{}$

$2 + 3 = 8 - \underline{}$

$5 = 8 - \boxed{3}$

$5 = 5$

Number on the left hand side of the equal to sign and right hand side of the equal to sign should be same after solving.

10. A. 0

⊘ Means '+'. Now replace it

$8 ⊘ 2$ means $8 + 2$

$10 ⊘ \underline{}$ means $10 + \underline{}$

$8 + 2 = 10 + \underline{}$

$10 = 10 + \boxed{0}$

$= 10$

Number on the left hand side of the equal to sign and right hand side of the equal to sign should be same after solving.

11. D. 0.

▢ Means +

$6 + 2 = 8 ▢ \underline{}$

$6 + 2 = 8 + \underline{}$

$8 = 8 + \boxed{0}$

$= 8$

Number on the left hand side of the equal to sign and right hand side of the equal to sign should be same after solving.

12. D. 6

$\triangle$ Means +

$10 \triangle 4$ means $10 + 4,$ $8 \triangle \underline{}$ means $8 + \underline{}$

$10 + 4 = 8 + \underline{}$

$14 = 8 + \boxed{6}$

$14 = 14$

Number on the left hand side of the equal to sign and right hand side of the equal to sign should be same after solving.

13. D. O.

    ⊘ Means -

    (Replace) 10 ⊘ 4 = 10 – 4 and

    (Replace) 6 ⊘ 6 = 6 – __

$$10 - 4 \ = 6 - \text{\_\_\_}$$
$$6 \ = \ 6 - \text{\_\_}$$
$$6 \ = \ 6 - \boxed{0}$$
$$6 \ = \ 6$$

Number on the left hand side of the equal to sign and right hand side of the equal to sign should be same after solving.

14. C. 3.

    ▭ Means '–' sign.

    (Replace) 8 ▭ 2 = 8 – 2

    (Replace) 9 ▭ __ means 9 – __

$$8 - 2 \ = 9 - \text{\_\_\_}$$
$$6 \ \ = \ 9 - \boxed{3}$$
$$6 \ \ = \ 6$$

Number on the left hand side of the equal to sign and right hand side of the equal to sign should be same after solving.

15. A. 5

    △ Means –

    9 △ 4 means 9 – 4

    10 △ __ means 10 – __

$$9 \ - 4 = 10 - \text{\_\_\_}$$
$$5 \ = 10 - \text{\_\_\_}$$
$$5 \ = \ 10 - \boxed{5}$$
$$5 \ = \ 5$$

16. A .12

Study the numbers carefully. Add 2 pattern OR 2 times table if you   know.

+ 2   +2   +2   +2   +2

2   4   6   8   10   ☐

17. D.

Observe carefully.

After standing rectangle comes the sleeping rectangle.

18. A.

After blank square comes a square with a triangle.

19. B.

Observe the pattern carefully.

20. B.

Observe the figure carefully and select the correct option.

21. A.

Observe the figure carefully and select the correct option.

22. C.

   The next figure will be rectangle.

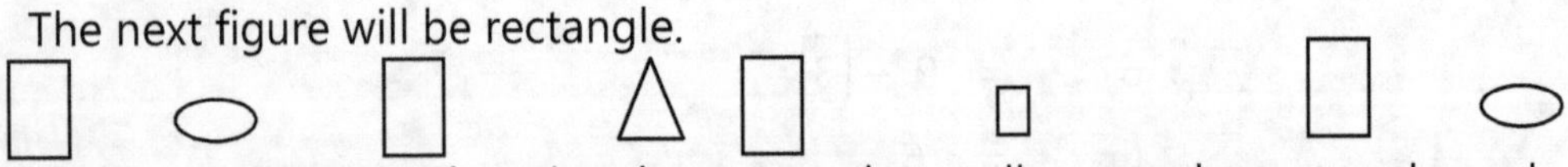

Rectangle,   oval, rectangle, triangle, rectangle, small rectangle, rectangle oval.

Observe carefully. So the next figure will be rectangle. ☐

23. A. R.

M is the first triangle. 7th triangle is S. Triangle S is after triangle R.

24. A.

Observe the figure carefully. Draw a straight line to make a triangle and you will get a proper shape.

25. B. 4

Number 1 has 1 square.

Number 2 has 2 square.

Number 3 has 3 squares.

So number 4 has 4 squares.

26. B.

Number 1 has one triangle.

Number 2 has two triangles.

Number 3 has three triangles.

Number 4 has four triangles.

Number 5 has five triangles.

27. B.

Observe the pattern and position of the circle.

28. B. 15

The pattern is to add 3

+ 3	+ 3	+3	3	
3	6	9	12	15

29. B. 19

Add 4

+4	+ 4	+ 4	+4	
3	7	11	15	19

30. B. 70, 74

Observe the numbers carefully.

Add 2

+2	+ 2	+ 2		+ 2	
66,	68,	**70**,	72,	**74**	

Chapter 7 : Time

1. B. 2 O' clock

Short hand is hour hand and long hand is minute hand. When hour hand is on 2 and minute hand is on 12. It is 2 O' clock

2. B. 4 O' clock

Short hand is hour hand and long hand is minute hand. When hour hand is on 4 and minute hand is on 12. It is 4 O' clock.

3. B. Morning

4. C. 7

There are 7 days in a week.

5. B. 7

When hour hand is on 7 and minute hand is on 12. It is 7 O' clock.

6. A. Hour hand

7. C. Tuesday

Monday, Tuesday , Wednesday, Thursday, Friday, Saturday, Sunday.

8. C. 12

9. B. 12 O' clock at night

10. D.

Short hand is hour hand and long hand is minute hand. When hour hand is on 8 and minute hand is on 12. It is 8 O' clock.

11. C.

3 O'clock is less than 6 O' clock.

12. B. 8 O' clock at night.

We have dinner at night.

13. A. Sunday.

Monday, Tuesday, Wednesday, Thursday, Friday, Saturday, Sunday .

14. B. October

January, February, March, April, May, June, July, August, September, October, November, December.

15. B.

One day has 24 hours.

16. A.

17. B.

One hour before 10 O'clock is 9 O'clock .

18. C.

Monday, Tuesday, Wednesday, Thursday, Friday , Saturday, Sunday.

19. B. October

    1)   January

    2)   February

    3)   March

    4)   April

    5)   May

    6)   June

    7)   July

    8)   August

    9)   September

    10) October

    11) November

    12) December

20. B. 15 July

    1st Friday is 1st July

    2nd Friday is 8th July

    3rd Friday is 15th July.

Chapter 8 : Measurement

1. B.

2. C.

3. C.

4. A. O

5. D . Q and S

6. C. L and N are same in size.

7. B.

    Vase B is smaller than vase X .

8. B. ruler

    We can measure length with the help of a ruler.

9. C. Weight

10. C. Weighing scale.

Solutions for Model Test Paper 1

1. C. 8 + 3 + 4

    Addition word problem

    Number of sweets I have   8

    + Number of sweets Rishika gave me   3

    + Number of sweets Anushka gave me   4

    Read the options carefully.

    8 + 3 + 4

2. C. 50 – 8 = 42

    Number of pens sold on Wednesday   50

    Number of less pens sold on Thursday   – 8

    Number of pens sold on Thursday.   42

    Subtraction word problem.

    Read the options carefully.

3. B. 91

    T   O

    7   2   (7 tens 2 ones.)

    + 1   9   (1 tens 9 ones)

    9   1

4. A. 5

    10 – 5   dots means

       10

    –   5

       5

5. B. 12-6

    15 – 9 = 6

    Search for an option whose answer is 6.

    Option A) 10 – 6 = 4 (incorrect)

    Option B) 12 – 6 = 6 (correct)

    Option C) 20 – 2 = 18 (incorrect)

6. D.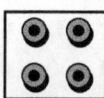

Equal means both the boxes should have same number of dots. Only option D has the same number of dots.

4 dots.

7. A. 98

8 ones means 8 in ones place and 9 tens means 9 in tens place.

T O

9 8

8. C. 80 + 4

84 means 8 tens OR 80

4 ones OR 4

80 + 4 = 84.

9. B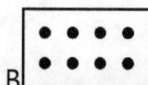

More than 7 but less than 9 means

7 < __ < 9

7 < 8 < 9

10. C. 09, 19, 90, 99

Read the numbers carefully

11. B.

Counting by 2's, means 2 times table OR add 2 to each number.

+2   +2   +2   +2   +2

0 = 2,   2 = 4,   4 = 6,   6 = 8 ,   8 = 10

12. B. ₹ 2 + ₹ 5

In India we don't have ₹ 6, ₹ 3, ₹ 4 coins .

Option A and option C shows ₹7 but we don't has these (₹6, ₹3, ₹ 4)coins in circulation.

Option B) ₹ 2 + ₹ 5 (we have ₹ 2 and ₹ 5 coins in circulation).

13. A. Eight 50 paisa coins

   ₹ 4 = 400 paisa.

   Search for an option which will give you ₹4 OR   400 paisa.

   Option A) Eight 50 paisa coins means eight coins of 50 paisa.

   50p + 50 p + 50 p + 50p + 50 p + 50 p + 50 p +50 p = 400 p = 4 ₹

   You can arrange it vertically and add.

   Option B) Five 50 paisa coins means 5 coins of 50 paisa.

   50p + 50 p + 50 p + 50 p + 50 = 250 p (incorrect option)

   Option C) Four 50 paisa coins means four coins of 50 paisa.

   50p + 50 p + 50 p + 50 p = 200p = ₹2 (incorrect option)

14. B.   ₹ 50.

   Ram pays ₹ 80 for two items. One is the 30 ₹ ball and the other item we have to find out.

   Out of ₹ 80 he spent ₹ 30.

$$\begin{array}{r} ₹\,80 \\ -\ ₹\,30 \\ \hline ₹\,50 \end{array}$$
   Bat is for ₹ 50

15. D ₹ 1, ₹ 2

   Janhavi wants to exchange her ₹ 3 with some coins. We have to search for an option which shows ₹ 3.

   Option A) two coins of 50 p makes 1 rupee

   50 p + 50p = 100 p = 1 Rupee

$$\begin{array}{r} +\ 1\ \text{Rupee} \\ \hline ₹\ 2\ ₹\,(\text{incorrect}) \end{array}$$

Option B) ₹2, ₹2

$$\begin{array}{r} ₹2 \\ + \ ₹\ 2 \\ \hline ₹4 \quad \text{(incorrect)} \end{array}$$

Option C) 50 p + 50 p = 100 p = 1 Rupee

    25 p + 25 p = 50 p

So ₹ 1 and 50 paisa. (incorrect)

Option D) ₹ 1 + ₹ 2 = ₹ 3 (correct)

16. C. 2

Cost of one toy car is ₹ 30. If she buys 2 toy cars she has to pay ₹ 30 + ₹ 30 = ₹ 60 .

Anushka has ₹ 70 with her.

Now after buying 2 cars she is left with 70 – 60 = ₹ 10.

She cannot buy one more toy car as the cost of one car is ₹ 30. She has ₹10 with her .

17. C. ₹ 35.

Cost of the bag   ₹ 75

Rujuta has   – ₹ 40

$$\hline ₹35$$

She needs ₹35 more to buy the bag.

        LETS CHECK

She has   ₹ 40

She needs more + ₹ 35

$$\hline ₹75 \text{ (amount that will help her buy the bag)}$$

18. C. 15

Rule or pattern is to add 3 OR 3 times table.

    +3   +3   +3   +3

    3,   6,   9,   12, ☐

19. B.   E

Square A is the last so square E will be the first.

Observe the figure carefully.

20. C. Four one rupee coins.

    ₹ 4 = 400 p

    Search for a set of money that will give you 400p OR ₹ 4.

    Option A) Five 50p coins means five coins of 50 paisa.

    50 p + 50 p + 50 p + 50 p + 50 = 250 p (incorrect option)

    Option B) Four 25 paisa coins means

    $\qquad$ 25 p + 25 p + 25 p + 25p = 100p = 1 rupee (incorrect option)

    Option C) Four one rupee coins

    1 + 1 + 1 + 1 = ₹ 4 OR 400p (correct)

21. B. 300

    ₹ 3 = 300 p

22. C. sphere

    Ball is a sphere, not cone or cylinder.

23. C. R

    Line P and line Q are slanting lines. Line S is vertical of standing lines. Line R is sleeping or horizontal line. (vertical and standing lines means the same, horizontal and sleeping lines means the same).

24. B. 42, 24, 12, 02.

    Read the numbers carefully.

    Remember 02 means 2

25. C. 80+6

    C's number is 86.

    Expanded form of 86 is 80+6.

26. C. 50

    Number that you are searching should be greater than 46 but less than 58.

    Option A) 59 is greater than 46, but also greater than 58 (incorrect)

    Option B) 45 is less than 46 (incorrect)

    Option C) 50 is greater than 46 but less than 58 (correct)

    Read and study the numbers carefully.

27. D. 0, 2, 4, 6, 8

Count by 2's means 2 times table OR add 2 to each number.

+2   +2   +2   +2

O = ☐2 ,   2 = ☐4 ,   4 = ☐6 ,   6 = ☐8

28. D. 7

8   +   ☐   = 15

8 Plus which number will be 15.

8   +   ☐7   = 15

29. B. 2

Subtraction word problem

Number of pencils Tanaya has   41

– Number of pencils she gave to Janhavi.   – 39

Number of pencils left with her   2

30. B. M

Count the sixth alphabet from right hand side.

31. A. ☐

1 circle, 2 triangles, 1 circle, 2 squares, 1 circle, 2 rectangles, 1 circle, 2 stars, 1 circle, 2 rectangle.

One rectangle is already there we need one more.

Study the figure carefully.

32. C. September.

33. A. Cup

We drink milk in a cup.

34. B. 6

Bundles of 10 pencils will make 60.

$$10 \ + 10 + 10 + 10 + 10 + 10 = 60$$

Each bundle carries 10 pencils.

35. A. 67

Addition word problem.

Number of figs Ved has	28
+ Number of figs Rishika has	+ 39
In all they have	67 figs.

Solutions for Model Test Paper 2

1. B. 82

Addition word problem.

Number of books Anushka has	33
Number of books Rujuta has	+ 49
Total books she has	82

2. C. 7

Bhoomi and Sai together picked up 21 apples. We know Sai picked up 14 apples.

So we subtract number of apples Sai picked up from the total to know how many Bhoomi picked up.

Subtraction word problem.

Together Bhoomi and Sai picked up	21
- Number of apples Sai picked up	− 14
Number of apples Bhoomi picked up.	7

3. B. 60+7

P's number is 67

Expanded form of 67 is 60 + 7.

4. C. 40

Addition word problem.

Number of tables	9
Number of bookshelves	+ 13
Number of beds	+ 18
Furniture sold in all	40

5. B. 16

   Subtraction word problem of money.

   Cost of the toy is ₹34.Janhavi gave ₹ 50 note. She gave more money. The shopkeeper will return her the extra money. He will take only ₹34.

$$
\begin{array}{r}
₹\,50 \\
-\,₹\,34 \\
\hline
₹\ 16
\end{array}
$$

6. C. E

7. B.5

   One bundle has 10 pens. So

   10 + 10 + 10 + 10 + 10 = 50

   5 bundles of pens will make 50 pens .

8. A. 09 ,90, 91 ,99

   Ascending or increasing order means small to big.

   Read the numbers carefully.

   Remember 09 means 9.

9. C.

   3 more than 49 is 49+3=52

   Search for an abacus which shows number 52.

   Option C) 5 tens and 2 ones = 52 (correct)

   5 beads in tens place and beads in ones place.

10. B. 98

    One more than 97 is 98,98 is less than 99.

    97   **98**   99

11. C.

    Counting by 3's means 3 times table OR Rule of adding 3.

    $$\overset{+3}{}\qquad \overset{+3}{}\qquad \overset{+3}{}\qquad \overset{+3}{}$$

    0 = 3,   3 = 6,   6 = 9,   9 = 12

12. B. 80+9

    Expanded form of 89 is 80+9

13. C. Squares are less than balls

Count the balls and squares carefully.

There are 5 balls.

There are 3 squares.

So squares are less than balls.

Read all the options carefully.

14. A. 34

4 ones means 4 in ones place .

3 tens means 3 in tens place.

  T O

  3 4

15. C. 9

9 ones means 9 in ones place. 0 tens means 0 in tens place.

    T O

    O 9

09 means 9.

16. C. 48

8 ones means 8 in ones place. 4 tens means 4 in tens place.

      T O

      4 8

17. C.

3 more than 6 means 3 + 6 = 9

Option C number line shows 6 + 3 = 9

18. C. 7 tens

3 tens means   30

4 tens means   + 40

           70 means 7 ten.

19. B. 68

3 more than 46 + 19 means add 3 to the sum of 46 and 19.

OR.

Add 3 + 46 + 19

$$
\begin{array}{r}
3 \\
+\ 46 \\
+\ 19 \\
\hline
68
\end{array}
$$

In addition we can change the arrangements of numbers.

20. D. None of these

$$
\begin{array}{ll}
2 \text{ tens means} & 20 \\
6 \text{ tens means} & +\ 60 \\
\hline
& 80 \ \text{ means 8 tens.}
\end{array}
$$

21. B. 3

8 – 3 = 5 means from total 8 balls cross out 3 balls, and then 5 balls are left. So cross out 3 balls

22. C.4.

Take away 2 means subtract 2 from 6.

   6 – 2 = 4

23. C.4.

10 – 6 dots means 10 – 6 = 4

24. C.3.

Count the balls carefully.

There are 8 blue balls.

There are 5 pink balls.

We need 3 more pink balls to make it equal to 8.

Let's check.

5 + **3** = 8

25. C. 9 – 5 = 4

5 less than 9 means subtract 5 from 9

9 – 5 = 4

Read all the options carefully.

26. B. 20 - 5

$19 - 4 = 15$

We have to search for an option which will give us 15.

Option A) $12 - 4 = 8$ (incorrect)

Option B) $20 - 5 = 15$ (correct)

Option C) $21 - 7 = 14$ (incorrect)

27. A. 6

Subtraction word problem.
Key words - went away, how many bugs left.
Number of bugs   21
Number of bugs went away   – 15
Number of bugs left.   06

28. D. Cube

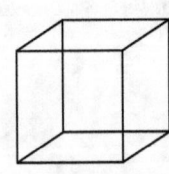 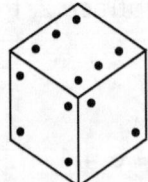

A dice has 6 faces.

29. D Cube

30. C. An ice-cream cone.

31. A .10

$\triangle$ Means   + so 6 $\triangle$ 4 will be 6 + 4

$\triangledown$ Means   – so 20 $\triangledown$ ___ will be 20 – ___

Now replace it with signs

6 △ 4 = 6 + 4

20 ▽ __ = 20 - __

6 + 4 = 20 − __

10   = 20 − [10]

10   = 10

Number on the left hand side of the equal to sign and right hand side of the equal to sign should be same after solving.

32. B. 3

    △   Means   + so 5 △ 3 will be 5 + 3

    ▽   Means   − So 11 ▽ ___ will be 11 − __

Now replace it with signs

  5 △ 3 = 5 + 3

  11 ▽ __ = 11 − __

  5 + 3 = 11 − __

   8   = 11 - [   ]

   8   = 8

Number on the left hand side of the equal to sign and right hand side of the equal to sign should be same after solving.

33. B.   Bell ₹30.

Tanaya has paid ₹ 50 for two items. She has bought a ball of ₹20 and one more item. Out of ₹ 50 she spent ₹ 20 for ball and the second items cost will be

50 − 20 = 30

Cost of the bell is ₹ 30.

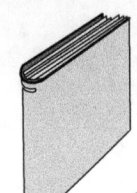

34.   B. book ₹ 30

Janhavi pays ₹ 80 for two items. She bought a pen of ₹ 50 and one more item. Out of ₹ 80, cost of pen is ₹ 50 and the second item costs

80 – 50 = 30

Cost of the book is ₹ 30.

35. B. Pencil box ₹ 40.

Anushka pays ₹ 70 for two items. She bought a bag of ₹ 30 and one more item. Out of ₹ 70, cost of bag is ₹ 30 and the second item costs.

70 – 30 = ₹ 40

Solutions for Model Test Paper 3

1. B. 2

    ☐ Means '+ 'So 7 ☐ 5 means 7 + 5

    10 ☐ means 10 + ___

    7 + 5 = 10 + ___

       12 = 10 + ☐ 2

       12 = 12

Number on the left hand side and right hand side of the equal to sign should be same after solving.

2. D. ☐

Observe the figure carefully.

The figure after a rectangle with circle is a blank rectangle.

3. C. 22

Pattern or rule is to add 3

      +3   +3   +3

      13   16   19   ☐ 22

4.   A. 15

45 + ___ = 60 (to solve we subtract)

60 – 45 = 15 (Sum - addend 1)

So 45 + **15** = 6.

80 – ___ = 65 (to solve we subtract)

80 – 65   = 15 (Minuend – difference)

80 – 15   = 65

Rule : In addition if any of the addend is missing we subtract.

5.   B. 8

Rule: In addition if sum is given and any of the addend is missing, we subtract.

22 + ___ = 30 (Sum - addend 1)

30- 22 = 8

Let's check   22 + **8** =30

40 – ___ = 32

40-32 = 8

Let's check 40 – **8** = 32

6.   A.   A

Box A has standing or horizontal line.

Box B has sleeping or vertical lines.

Box C and D has slanting lines.

7.   A. 10

10 < 40

8.   B. Five one rupee coins

Search from set of money that shows ₹ 5 OR 500 p

Option A : Two 50 paisa coins

50p + 50p = 100p = 1 Rupee (incorrect)

Option B : Five one rupee coins .

₹ 1 + ₹ 1 + ₹ 1 + ₹ 1 + ₹ 1 = 5 ₹ OR 500 p (Correct)

Option C : Four 25 paisa coins.

25 p + 25 p + 25 p + 25 p = 100 p = 1 Rupee (incorrect)

Option D: Five ten paisa coins .

10p + 10p + 10p + 10p + 10p = 50p (incorrect)

9.   B. 50 p, 50 p, 50 p ,50 p

Cost of the balloon is ₹ 2 OR 200 P

Option a : 25p + 25p + 25p = 75p (incorrect)

Option b : 50p + 50p + 50p + 50p = 200p = 2 ₹ (Correct)

Option c : ₹ 1 (incorrect)

10. B. 30

Cost of the toy is ₹ 45. Anushka has ₹ 15 only.

She has less money. She needs some more money. She needs

₹ 45 – ₹ 15 = ₹ 30

Let's check ₹ 15 + ₹ 30 = ₹ 45

11. C. ₹ 2, ₹ 1, 50 p, 50 p, 50 p, 50 p

Tanya wants to exchange ₹ 5 with some coins. Search for a set of money that will give ₹ 5 OR 500p.

Option A: 50 p + 50 p = 1 Rupee

+   50 p + 50 p = 1 Rupee

+   2 Rupee
                      _____
                              4 Rupees (incorrect)

Option B: 50 p + 50 p = 1 rupee [100 p]

25 p + 25 p + 25 p + 25 p = 1 rupee [100 p]
                      _____
                              2 rupees [200 p] (incorrect)

Option B :   ₹ 2

                              + ₹ 1

        50 p + 50 p = 1 Rupee

+   50 p + 50 p = 1 Rupee
                      _____
                              5 Rupees (Correct)

12. C. ₹ 68.50

$$
\begin{array}{r}
₹\ 50 \\
+\ ₹\ 10 \\
+\ ₹\ 5 \\
+\ ₹\ 2 \\
+\ ₹\ 1 \\
\hline
₹\ 68 + 50\ p
\end{array}
$$

We separate rupees and paisa by a dot. So we write it as ₹ 68.50

13. C .50 p, 50 p, ₹ 1, ₹ 1

₹ 3 = 300 P.

Search for 300 p OR ₹ 3

Option A: 50 p + 50 p = ₹ 1

$$
\begin{array}{r}
+\ ₹\ 1 \\
\hline
2\ ₹\ \text{(incorrect)}
\end{array}
$$

Option B: 25 p + 25 p + 25 p + 25 p = 1 rupee [100 p]

$$
\begin{array}{r}
+\ 1\ \text{rupee} \\
\hline
2\ \text{rupees\ (incorrect)}
\end{array}
$$

Option C :   50p + 50 p = 100 p = ₹ 1

$$
\begin{array}{r}
+\ ₹\ 1 \\
+\ ₹\ 1 \\
\hline
₹\ 3\ \text{(correct)}
\end{array}
$$

14. C.   ⟶ ₹ 40

Hrishika pays ₹ 90 for 2 items. Item one is a  for ₹ 50 and she bought one more item.

Out of ₹ 90, cost of  is ₹ 50, so the second item will be for ₹ 90 – 50 = ₹ 40 .

Option C : aeroplane costs ₹ 40

15. D. Four 50 paise coins.

   ₹ 2 = 200 p

   Search for a set of money that will give you 200 p OR ₹ 2 .

   Option A : Ten 10 paisa coins

   10 p + 10 p + 10 p + 10 p + 10 p + 10 p + 10 p + 10 p + 10 p + 10 p = 100p = 1 Rupee (incorrect)

   Option B) Five 50 p coins.

   50 p + 50 p + 50 p + 50 p + 50 p = 250p (incorrect)

   Option C : Four 25 paisa coins.

   25 p + 25 p + 25 p + 25 p= 1 rupee [100 p] (incorrect)

   Option D : Four 50 p coins .

   50p + 50p + 50p + 50p = 200p = ₹ 2 (correct)

16. C. 7tens

   3 tens means 30

   + 4 tens means 40
   _____

   70 means 7 tens

   Read the options carefully.

17. B. 5th point.

   Janhavi's first step is on number 2 and then she jumps 3 steps. So 2 + 3 = 5. She will reach number 5.

18. C.

    14 + 5 = 19. We have to search for an abacus which shows number 19.

    Option C. One bead in tens place so 1 tens and nine beads in ones place. So 9 ones.

    T O

    1 9

19. C. 7 – 3 = 4

    Observe the number line carefully. It shows a jump from 0 to 7 means 7, and 3 jumps backwards means minus 3. So 7 – 3 = 4

    Read all the options carefully

20. C. 38

    $$\begin{array}{r} 8 \text{ tens} = 80 \\ - 4 \text{ tens } 2 \text{ ones} = 42 \\ \hline 38 \end{array}$$

21. C. 23

    $$\begin{array}{r} 6 \text{ tens } 2 \text{ ones} = 62 \\ 3 \text{ tens } 9 \text{ ones} = - 39 \\ \hline 23 \end{array}$$

    62 – 39 = 23

22. C.

    Big rectangle ▯ = 10 , Small rectangle ☐ = 5

    So ▯ =10 ☐ – 5☐ = 5

    10 – 5 = 5

23. D. 19- 12 = 7

    We have to search for an abacus that shows 7.

    Option d shows number 7.

    (Be careful option a shows 7 beads in tens place = 70. Don't get confused. You are in search of 7 beads in ones place.)

24. A. 12

Subtraction word problem.

Number of balloons   21
Number of balloons bursted.   − $\underline{9}$
                                            12

25. B. 9

Take away 3 means. Subtract 3 from 12.

12 − 3 = 9

26. A. 5

Yellow balls = 9

Green ball =   4

Count the balls carefully. We need 4 more green to make it equal to yellow balls.

27. C. 25 - 8

20 − 3 = 17. Search for an option which shows number 17 after subtracting.

Option A. 14 − 4 = 10

Option B. 30 − 23 = 7

Option C. 25 − 8 = 17

28. B.2

6 + **2** = 8

29. B.

4 more than 8 means 4+8

4 + 8 = 12

Option b. number line shows 8 + 4 = 12

30. B. 51

4 more than 33 + 14 means add 4 to the sum of 33 + 14

33 + 14 + 4 = 51

31. C. both A and B

    Addition word problem

    Number of sweets Rujuta has   26

    Number of sweets Bhoomi has   +   11

    Number of sweets Veda has   +   13

    Read all the options carefully.

    Option A: 26+11+13

    Option B: 13+11+26 . Both the options means the same.

    Addition rule: We can change the arrangement of numbers in addition. Answer will not change by changing the arrangement of numbers.

32. C.

    $14 + \underline{\mathbf{3}} = 17$

33. B. 35+23=58

    Count the beads carefully and write the numbers.

    $35 + 23 = 58$

34. B. 5 + 4

    On adding 5 + 4 we get 9.

    $5 + 4 = 9$

35. C. 23 − 9 = 14

    Subtraction word problem.

    Number of dolls sold on Thursday   23

    Number of less dolls sold on Friday.   −   9

    Number of dolls sold on Friday.   14

Notes